Knockouts

Time Rope

They were strangers. They met by chance under the tree with its mysterious hanging rope.
Tod, Fee and Roller.
But their fates are linked together.

LONGMAN GROUP LIMITED
Longman House
Burnt Mill, Harlow, Essex CM20 2JE, England and
Associated Companies throughout the World.

First published 1986
ISBN 0 582 25092 7 (paper)
0 582 25088 9 (cased)

Produced by Longman Group (F.E.) Limited
Printed in Hong Kong

Time Rope 1

Time Rope

Robert Leeson

Longman

Thanks to Fred Leeson, for advice and help.

Contents

1 Time Annexe

In a small, darkened room on Level Three of the Time Annexe, a girl stirred in her sleep. Her dreaming grew more excited.

Outside in the main control chamber, the face of one wall dissolved into light. An image formed – the inner room, the bed and the girl's long slim body as she turned restlessly.

The level hum and tick of recording instruments changed. A single pulse of sound rose a fraction above the others. The change was minute but it reached through a hundred metres of concrete, metal and earth to the surface.

Two men in green jackets walked along the concrete ways among low, grey buildings. The taller one, thin, grey-haired, heard the pulse as it reached the instrument packet clipped into his pocket. He said nothing but increased his pace. The small, square younger man had to hurry to keep up with him.

They entered the first block, with its dingy, slab and metal walls. The young scientist sniffed. The older one grinned.

'You're not impressed with our famous Centre?'

'Reminds me of an old 20th century heliport.'

'Right first time. That's what it was.'

They hastened down poorly-lit, windowless corridors, the younger man matching his colleague's stride.

'Why?' he asked. 'This Centre must have more money than every other Research establishment put together.'

'Our Controller has his own ideas about what money is for. Staff facilities ground level. Research below ground. You'll see.'

The grey-haired man paused by a door set in the wall, thumbed a button and spoke briefly into a panel. He turned.

'That's how he likes it. The Centre attracts less attention if it looks like a dump on the outside.'

The door opened on a lift, gleaming white and silver. It closed behind them and they plunged down, the level numbers flickering. Below more corridors, smooth-walled, pale, cool, green.

'Someone likes green.'

'Relaxing. You need it.'

The older man's pace increased.

'Are they hot on time-keeping?'

'Time is all we have to work with here. But no, I'm hurrying because you may be in for a little excitement on your first day in the Annexe.'

Another brief pause as the blank wall ahead opened, and they were in the control chamber. The young scientist stared at the wall screen, the sleeping girl.

'The Sleeping Beauty,' he murmured.

'You know that story. I'm amazed.'

'All my generation is not pig ignorant.'

The grey-haired man smiled. 'Maybe we'll get on well together after all. That will be –' he paused 'important.' He pointed to the screen. But there was no need. His new colleague was staring fascinated as the girl turned again, and her face, partly masked with strands of fair hair, became visible. The eyes were closed, and under the light covers, her breasts rose and fell swiftly.

'Yes, indeed, something is going to happen.'

At a touch of a switch, the opposite wall bloomed into light and colour. A bedroom, a sleeping girl, turning restlessly. Both men glanced rapidly from one image to another, then the younger one burst out.

'That's – wait – a different room, a different

bed. But the same girl.'

'Try the close up,' his senior commanded.

He stepped to the control panel, hesitated, then selected a switch. The second girl's face suddenly filled the screen.

'No. The hair has auburn in it. The nose, more turned up. But that eyebrow, there's the same, slight kink in it.'

'The same, and not the same, eh?'

'Sisters.'

A shake of the head. 'The girl next door is an only child.'

The two men stared at each other.

'The difference between them is over forty years. The difference between 1988 and 2034.'

'Yes, I see that, now, the furnishing, the bed-clothes. But there's nothing special in that, is there. We've had almost complete retro-record for years now.' The young man laughed. 'You've just homed in on her mother, or her aunt …'

'Come on. Don't disappoint me. We are not spending time and money on primitive scanning. Our interest is not *what* people did fifty years, five hundred years ago. We know that. Our study is how they thought and felt. We intend to know not what they did, but why.'

Now the young scientist was excited. 'But

how do you monitor ...?'

'We do not monitor, she does.' His colleague gestured to the first screen with its sleeping girl. 'She knows what that girl is doing all those years ago, she thinks, feels, experiences it all along with her.'

He turned his grey head from the study of the screen.

'That is the discovery on which our work is based, that makes retro-record as obsolete as 1980s television. Each human heing hands on not just a package with body shape, skin colour, hair, disease or health, but the memory record of everything they have done, everything that happens to them.'

'That record, excitement, fear, love, hate, can be tapped. You can become those people that were you in the past.'

The young man stood, silent, his eyes turning from one screen to another. Then he gestured towards the door leading to the side room.

'So she is not here and now with us, but then and there in the past.'

'Her mind is stretched between the present and the past.'

'But the dangers. Suppose she cannot get back.'

The grey-haired man eyed his colleague for a moment, then said quietly. 'There are casualties. As there were with the first astronauts. Not death, but something worse in its way, permanent – not amnesia, not loss of memory, but permanent memory, a life with no present . . .'

'And no future . . .'

A shake of the head.

'So that is why the top secrecy. That is why the Controller's personal interest.'

'My friend, Martell, our Controller has an eye on every project. You of all people ought to know that.'

The young man stared.

'Why . . .?' he began to say. His colleague ignored the question and went on. 'The Government is very interested, too.'

'But I thought the Centre was private.'

A quick laugh. 'Don't be naïve. Everything in our society is private. That is state policy. But some private enterprises get special Government attention, and the Centre is one. Only those directly involved know the Centre is under Cabinet supervision.'

He put a warning hand on the other's arm.

'Don't forget that. This is research of the utmost importance. The aim is simple, but far-reaching.'

He paused, then spoke more quietly, yet firmly.

'Know who you were, understand who you are, decide what you will be.'

2 Time Rope

The older scientist swung round to the second screen and pointed.

'This is the cause of our excitement. We are about to Return.'

The younger man was baffled. But he said nothing, but instead watched the screen. With a single, graceful movement, the girl had swung from the bed. Standing, she threw off the light night dress and walked naked to the door. She paused, carefully opened it, slipped through and as carefully closed it behind her.

'Very quiet lady. Considerate.'

The other slowly shook his head. 'Not considerate, I think. Though if you notice from the bedside clock, it is only six in the morning. I think she has something to do which she wishes others not to know.'

The door opened on screen and the girl, clad in jeans and tee-shirt, hair tied back loosely behind her ears, came back into the bedroom. Suddenly she sank onto the bed, bent and put her head between her hands. A moment passed. She remained there.

And on Screen One the other girl became more agitated in her sleep.

'What next?'

'Wait. We can only wait. This work, my friend, is mainly waiting. But then, the excitement of a Return makes up for many patient hours.'

'So our Annexe Director will be happy?'

'That I doubt.'

'Why?'

'Because this Return is happening early, too early. It was scheduled for ten days' time, when, as it happens, by one of those coincidences which belong with politics, not science, we have a Very Important Visitor to the Centre. The Prime Minister, no less.'

'I see. A well-timed success, more funds.'

'You learn quickly. In this business, like every other, money is power and power is money. The Controller of this Centre is a very, very ambitious man. Time Annexe, like every other project here, has to fit into his plan.'

'But can you decide, just like that, when someone Returns?'

'No, that is decided by what is happening to them, in the past. But their return can be delayed. They can be held, in the Neutral Zone – a place where there is neither past, present or future.'

'And that can be dangerous?'

'The longer anyone is there, the more dangerous. Just how dangerous we do not know, for we have never held anyone there for so long. Look.'

The middle wall now dissolved into a third image. A moving image, first buildings, then a narrow strip of water, a canal, and beyond it a long view of desolate landscape, rough grass and stunted trees and bushes. As the image changed, the picture was clouded as if by mist, cold and swirling, then in the distance appeared the vague shapes of low buildings.

'But – that's the Centre,' gasped the young scientist.

'As it was, forty years ago. Built on an area of 20th century industrial dereliction so bad that for decades no construction was allowed, for fear of subsidence, the complete collapse of the land, into the holes and tunnels of generations of uncontrolled mining. A place where nothing happened, nothing at all. An ideal place for a Neutral Zone, don't you think? An ideal place to begin in a small way, research into Time.'

The image shifted again, back to the canal bank. On the edge of the water stood an oak tree, squat, gnarled, old and powerful, with a single, jagged branch that stretched out over the water. As the mist cleared slowly, the picture focussed on the branch. Hanging from it, swinging gently to and fro across the surface of the water was a rope. The older scientist looked at his colleague's puzzled expression.

'A rope. A kid's plaything. Do you remember the thrill of childhood dreams, of swinging through the air, swinging without effort, endlessly swinging, to and fro.'

'This, friend, is something beyond dreams – a Time Rope. Our time track is laid to catch that point in space and time. It is like a one strand web to catch a single fly.'

He pointed to the wall of the adjoining room.

'To free herself from that past life, she must bring that other girl to the rope.'

'Then the girl from the past must make the Time Swing?'

'Into the Neutral Zone and no further. Then she, too, will return to her own time …'

'And, remember nothing?'

'She will have a memory of the future. You know the old stories. There are tales of people who wandered into fairy hills and stayed a hundred years, and came back to find less than a night had passed. That is Time Rope.'

'And when our girl returns?'

'She will have a memory of the past, a series of recorded dreams with every thought and feeling as if she had experienced them herself.'

'But while she is in the Neutral Zone?'

'She will not know if she belongs to past or future.'

'And there lies the risk?'

'There lies the risk.' The grey-haired man pointed to Screen Two. The girl in jeans stood up determinedly, and tip-toed across the bedroom floor.

'And there is another side to the risk – a well – political one. Our volunteer – as you know – is no ordinary lady.'

'But I ...' the young man started to speak, hesitantly, when he saw a quick flash of bafflement in the older scientist's face. He turned away hastily, baffled in his turn.

The two men carried on their work in silence. Gradually they forgot about each other and concentrated on the screen, and the girl.

3 Fee

Fee silently closed her bedroom door and went quietly down the passage. The thick carpet muffled her footsteps, but still she went with breath held tight, as she had done when very small and engaged on some secret errand. She was nearly eighteen and she was leaving home.

The note addressed to her father, which she had taken from her pocket, said only: *Need time to think. Going for a few days. Please don't follow me. Say I'm ill.*

A few days? Was she trying to convince her father or herself?

Would she come back?

That she could not answer. She would not think more than the hours just ahead. For eighteen years her life had run its smooth, well-planned course. Today it could be that the rest of her life would be planned. Her father planned well. He was a genius for planning. His schemes always worked. And she was one of his schemes.

For eighteen years that had been true. And

she had known it, and accepted it. She'd done what she wanted, hadn't she? Any interest, any study, any sport, nothing had been denied her. Each wish became reality even as she wished it. Her father had never said 'no' to her. She had never said 'no' to any wish of his. There had been no need, until now.

Silently opening and closing another door, she entered the gallery that ran the whole length of the rear of the great house. Through the long windows she looked out over lawns, walls, tree-lined avenues, parkland, then in the distance to the waste-land and moors beyond.

That waste-land, pitted and scarred with the crumbling iron and brickwork of generations of buildings, was their wealth. Twenty square miles of devastation. Coal, steel, shipping, aluminium, canning, electronics, computers, step by step each generation of Hordens had planned, and won, and moved and changed.

In a flash a picture registered in her mind. Her own face beneath a strident newspaper headline: *Fiona, No 1 Heiress. Who'll be the Lucky Man?*

And another, flashing in and out of her mind more quickly: *Royal Guest for Shy Fiona.*

Shy? Was she shy? She did not really know. No one came close enough for her to feel shyness. But 'shy' Fiona seemed suitable. Virginal. She felt a jolt in her mind at the word and its truth. A well-preserved specimen. Lifetime guarantee for the right man.

But she'd accepted all her father's plans so far – they suited her. Why not this one?

She swung from the window to face the panelled wall opposite with its rows of Horden portraits, collar and tie, lace, velvet, wigs, riding crops, sword hilts stretching away into the half dark of the further end of the gallery, stretching away in time. Half way down she found the one she sought and looked again at it, more closely than ever.

Margaret, Lady Horden, 1765–1793. Poor Meg. Died young. Died out of her mind. Mad Meg. It was just two weeks ago one of her friends (one of her father's spies, too) had said 'Look Fee. She could be your twin.'

She had run to look in the mirror. And it was so. It was her own face, changing, that now matched Lady Meg's. A cold-hot feeling swept through her. Dying mad at 28 – ten years to go. But why?

Plucking up courage she asked her father. He was home briefly from a trip abroad, new plans in his brief-case, new schemes in his mind.

His eyebrows raised mockingly. 'Not you,

Fee. You are the sanest woman I know. The idea of you doing anything crazy is beyond my imagination.'

'Lady Margaret was a very clever lady, very active. A woman of talent. She was just eighteen, about to marry. A terrible accident, her father . . . ,' he paused, 'the shock was too much, they say ... her mind went . . .'

He looked out of the study window.

'It was an – arranged marriage. But ... not a tragedy though. Her husband took care of her, and her child. Very few outside the family knew the full story ...'

Suddenly she thought. And you are not telling me the whole story. But that was a new kind of thought for her. And she kept silent.

But that night, in her dreams, she saw Mad Meg. She came close, so close their faces were like face and mirror. Then Meg seemed to pass inside her and she woke up alarmed in the darkness, body streaming with sweat. Next day, she looked around in the library for some book, record, journal or other that might tell her more.

'What on earth do you want with all that, Fee?'

Her friend stood behind her.

Fee turned and told a lie, so well worked out she surprised herself. But she gave up the search.

Too much interest in anything, she had learnt, and her friend would report it back to her father. She kept her growing, passionate interest in Mad Meg to herself. And she suddenly realised that for the first time in her eighteen years she had a private life. That was what lies were for. Fee, who had always been outspoken, innocent, frank, became devious and crafty in her secret mind. She began to find ways of avoiding her friend, avoiding the house staff, to spend seconds, moments, now and then an hour, by herself.

And in these quiet moments, even in daylight, she began to see Meg, walking towards her, sitting by her side, once riding alongside her across the park. She wanted to talk to her, but Meg would not answer.

But Meg was telling her something, it seemed.

When her father came home that weekend and told her his latest plan, his plan for her, she had said nothing. That night in her dreams Meg came and passed into her and in the morning when she woke she knew what she was going to do – what she was not going to do.

Now in the grey of this early dawn she stood again and looked at Meg's portrait, just for a moment, before moving on quietly and swiftly, out of the gallery and by the narrow spiral staircase that led down to the coach house and the stable yard. If anyone saw her now she would be taking an early morning ride. That letter would not be opened by her father's secretary until nine o'clock. So she had nearly three hours.

No one saw her go. She jog-trotted across the park and climbed the wall just out of sight of the keeper's lodge. Leaping down on the other side, she slid down grassy banks and picked her way through bushes to the canal bridge. Here the road to town ran past. But she turned her back on it and faced the open country. Now she ran swiftly along the tow path, under warehouse and factory walls which soon gave out into allotment patches, smallholdings, orchards, fields.

Soon, on the farther bank, she saw the end of the estate wall and then her way took her through the waste-land. The canal which had seen coke and iron-ore laden barges follow one another like trains, was empty now, with broken banks half repaired, clumps of elder and willow, dank weed and thigh-deep grass.

She ran on strongly, a mile, two miles. Behind her, town, estate wall all vanished. She was in open, derelict, wasted countryside, with no one near. She ran on, not knowing where she might be heading for but certain of one thing. This was one action in her life she had decided for herself. No one had planned it, unless it were Mad Meg.

She slowed down. Now she was both hungry and thirsty and the sun was climbing. It was a glorious day. Her father had planned it well. TV and press cameras would make the most of the scene on the lawns. 'Shy Fiona waiting for ...'

Shy Fiona wanted a drink. Should she risk turning off at the next bridge and stopping for ten minutes at a lonely pub? No one knew her round here. Though everyone, everywhere, had seen her face. Would they recognise her in these grubby jeans and shirt, her hair tied back, not curving over her eyes? She'd risk it.

It was then, as she rounded a bend in the canal and came clear of a massive clump of bushes that she saw the tree, and beyond it the level scrubland rising gently through heat haze to the purple moors beyond. And from the tree hung the rope, swinging gently. Half across the water it hung, near and yet out of reach.

On impulse, she ran back, snapped off a branch of elder, twigs leaves and all. Taking it by the twig end she swung it round and round her head then let drive with the thicker end against the rope. It shook violently and then began a slow, widening circle round towards her. As it swung so it seemed to gather speed and flew by above her head as she ducked in alarm. Then she leapt and caught at it, her feet running on the sloping grass shelf and across the broken tow path.

In the next second, with a jar that shook breath from her chest, she was in the air, swinging and circling towards the other bank. Her speed increased. Instinctively she drew up her knees to add force, and then, too late, saw that she was heading now full tilt towards the broad, rough-barked trunk of the tree.

She trust violently with her legs and feet as if to break the force of the impact as she crashed into the tree. But felt nothing. There was nothing. The swing went on, and on. Tree, canal, waste-land, sky and sun had vanished. There was only light dark, light and dark again. Light and dark and numbing, numbing cold, that went on and on until she could take no more. Her grasp on the rope weakened and then she was falling, falling.

She struck rough ground, grass, stones, brambles, rolled and rolled. Then came to rest, lying half winded, half stunned.

Slowly she opened her eyes. She still felt the

harsh ground beneath her, but there was not pain. She had been bruised and cut in her fall, she knew, but there was no mark, no blood. There was nothing, nothing around her, but a white mist that clung to her body and stretched away and away.

She struggled to her feet and turned. The canal, the tree must be behind her, she thought, but how far away? The turning of her body took enormous effort, as though she were paralysed with sleep, as though she were dreaming. And her body felt heavy and frozen. She tried to walk, but her legs would not move apart. She took each one in turn and willed it to move, but it would not. She must be injured, somehow, in her fall, but how, where? For there was no pain, no feeling. She sank down.

Her head began to spin and through it ran, like a crazy film, pictures – home, school, holidays, Father, friends, reporters, police, soldiers, like a non-stop news report with her at its centre, then suddenly the film whirred into blankness and silence. Her body was growing colder, her head lighter, emptier.

It was then she saw the boy. At first faintly, in part outline, as if a cursor drew him on a computer screen – the outer shape and then, slowly the inner details. She stared. Was he in her mind or in the world outside? He moved, rising slowly, shakily from the ground to stand over her. How old was he? No more than sixteen perhaps, but small, like one of the stable lads. The face – pale, sharp-chinned, sullen. She did not know him. Then the eyes, dark, coal-dark, framed in incredibly deep black eyelashes and eyebrows. Such a mixture of ugliness and beauty she had never seen before.

'Who are you?' she breathed.

His lips moved, but she could hear nothing.

4 Tod

Tod woke at dawn. The pain woke him – ribs, stomach muscles, head, back, each part of his body had its own pain. He had slept wildly. He remembered people coming in from hour to hour, putting back sheets he had thrown off his hot, delirious body. Then they gave him a needle and he had dropped into a deep hole of sleep in the small hours.

Then memory came back. The fight, the manic fight through the top floor of the hostel, crashing over beds, chairs, cupboards, five of them on to him, punching, beating, kicking. But who had started it? He had. He knew that. He could have killed them all – especially Kirky.

Then he knew. He heard again the crunch and splintering crash as Kirky's body flew against and broke through the bannister rails, the crushing thud of it hitting the stairs and rolling, rolling. And Hicks shrieking.

'He's topped Kirky. The little bastard's topped Kirky.'

Tod lay back on the pillows, a sudden fierce satisfaction rushing like a wave through him. Yes he had. Yes he had. Kirky was off his back, now, for good and all.

Kirky was the boss. He ran that hostel, whatever that fat, oily warden Jamieson said or thought. 'In care', that's what the council called it. 'In care.' Oh yes, Kirky took care of everybody in the hostel. They were all there because foster parents or real parents had given up on them.

Tod knew all about it. His parents had given up on him before he even knew them – killed in a car crash. What you never have, you never miss. Oh yes. Well you can train yourself. Tod felt sorry for all the decent, caring, misguided couples that had tried to make sense of him. He'd tried, but it wasn't on. They couldn't give him what he wanted. That wasn't their fault. Wasn't his. So back he'd gone each time, to the hostel, where Kirky took care of him.

Kirky wasn't all that big. Hicks had the weight. And the others all joined in because if you didn't, you were a marked man for next time round when it was somebody else's turn. Kirky ruled by fear and humiliation, and took sadistic pleasure in every detail of the many trials and punishments he put his subjects through.

Tod was not afraid of Kirky. He was not even afraid of Hicksie. Tod was afraid of nobody. When you're on your own from three upwards you either give in to everyone or you find out how to stand up for yourself. That's where he got the name, Tod. His real name was Steven, Steven Morris. And he had one middle name he kept quiet, Sebastien. How he knew it, he didn't know. Why he should have been christened that, he didn't know. At least he hadn't known, until last night.

Last night was when he had begun to find out some of the answers to some of the questions about himself he had tried to answer. The strange thing was that it was Kirky who had given him the answers. Before Kirky had started, all he had known about himself was that he was an orphan from a baby, that his grandad had looked after him a bit, then he'd been taken into care.

Until Kirky had decided it was time for some detective work. So last night, when the warden was off duty, and the deputy warden, a nice girl, but very young and inexperienced, was distracted by some cock and bull story about one of the younger lads being sick, Kirky had broken into the office. He had done it very smoothly. He was talented was Kirky and had a career in crime ahead of him. And he had come back with a bunch of files.

Then after lights out, when the warden and deputy were out of the way, Kirky had put on the lamp over his bed and called the others together. They came, half eager, half fearfully, because they guessed what Kirky was going to reveal. Tod knew what it was all about – it was about making him eat dirt.

The first laugh came when Kirky read out Tod's full name. The others punched each other and fell about.

'Sebastien,' said Hicks. 'With a name like that, he's got to be gay, hasn't he?'

Kirky moved swiftly. He reached out and gripped Tod's jaw, forcing his face up. 'Oh yes, that's very smart, Hicksie, I'd never thought of that. Just look at those eyelashes. And we never knew, never suspected. We'll have to see about that won't we, boys.'

Tod jerked his head away and reached suddenly for the sheaf of papers in Kirky's hands, but Kirky was quicker. As he snatched it back he nodded to Hicks and two others, who seized Tod from the back, forcing his arms under his shoulder-blades.

'Now Sebastien, be a good boy and listen. This is your life. Ooooh. This is interesting now.

This explains a lot. His grandad, the dirty old sod, married a Spanish bird. Amazing what people'll do isn't it? I always thought there was a touch of the nig nog to our Sebastien – poor little bastian – get it Toddy?'

Tod allowed his body to go limp. If once dim Hicks and the others slackened their grip, he'd get free. And he knew what he'd do. First he'd take that file and tear it into shreds. Then he'd ...

'Poor old Granddad,' went on Kirky. 'He got lumbered with little Sebastien when his parents were killed in a car kwash.'

'Aaah,' said the others, 'poor little bastian.'

'The old boy went a bit funny in the head when his old woman died. And when the nice men from the council came to take little Sebastien away, the old devil he smashed the place up.'

The circle of lads around Kirky was quiet. Something in the story had got through to them. This wasn't funny any more.

It was then that Tod seized his chance. Lunged forward butting Kirky in the face, slipped his tormentors' grasp, snatched the file and was on the landing when the others caught up with him. Abandoning his plan to shred the file, Tod had settled for killing Kirky.

The bedroom door opened. A nurse came in, a broad shouldered, dark-suited man behind her. The Law. Tod knew in the instant, and just as quickly closed his eyes and lay slack in the bed. He felt the nurse come close to him, the hospital smell grew more sharp to his nostrils. She took his wrist. Her fingers were cool.

'Not just yet, I'm afraid. But when he comes to, I think you'll be able to talk to him.'

Their voices faded, the door closed. Tod's mind worked at speed. He was not, not going to be given a going over about Kirky. He'd done Kirky and that was it. Otherwise, why were the Law here. And he was not going to answer questions about Kirky. The thoughts circled in his feverish mind, as he slid from the bed and headed for the door. At the first step, his legs failed him. He found himself on all fours, head swimming. But he clung to the bed and hauled himself up to the foot where his jacket and jeans hung over a chair. The next steps were easier. The door open a fraction and he saw the passage outside was empty.

Now there was no more hesitation. In a matter of seconds he had the sash window up and had rolled over the sill into the dusty shrubbery outside. As he headed for the gate, he thought he heard shouting behind him. But he did not look back. He had run from authority too many times in the past. Looking back was fatal.

At the driveway he halted, zipped his jacket up to the throat, stuck his hands into his jeans pockets and walked past the gate house. The gatekeeper noticed the lad with his black-bruised, pale face go by. But did not remember it until the police questioned him later that morning.

Tod dodged through the town, leaning now and then on walls to get breath and allow the sudden rushes of faintness to drain from head and body. Now and then he slid into shop doorways as a police car went by. That was funny. Why all the Law about at this time in the morning? He counted five, six squad cars, not rushing about, but cruising. Were they after him? Couldn't be, could they. Not that soon.

But as he made his slow way across town, he began to have doubts. Once, at a corner, he heard a car engine easing down alongside him.

'Just a minute, lad ...'

The familiar tones sent him dodging round the corner and staggering along a narrow pavement. High walls rose above him. Warehouses, factories. He heard the police car turn, put on pace. He ran on, then came up sharp. It was a dead end. The street ended in a brick wall. Even then he did not hesitate. He flung himself at a dustbin by the brickwork, stamped his foot on the lid and grabbed for the top of the wall in a wild jerking leap. He was over in one movement and dropping to land half on his knees on rough, flinty ground. Rolling, he felt his feet and trouser-legs in water. He was on the canal tow path. Well, they couldn't get at him here, could they?

Paying no heed to the fresh blood that trickled down inside his jeans, he set off at an awkward run along the canal bank, heading along the warehouse fronts, heading out of town.

Two hours painful walking, jogging run, breathless resting, and he was clear of the buildings and out in open country.

The sun was high in the white-blue sky, when he turned the bend in the canal and saw the tree and the rope for the first time.

5 Time Annexe

Deep below ground in the Time Annexe, the two researchers sat in silence at the control panel, and stared at the screen on the centre wall. The other screens were blank now. All attention was on the Neutral Zone. And now they had been silently joined by others on the team. After a while one spoke.

'Well, there's an improbability for you. Two flies on a one strand web.'

Medway, the grey-haired man, stroked his chin.

'It can happen. It has happened before.'

'But what now?' demanded Jonas, his young colleague.

'First we shall wait. And observe. If it is by chance, if this boy has blundered in, then he will blunder out. The Neutral Zone is an unwelcoming place.'

'They are trying to talk to each other.'

'They cannot, not yet. The time interval between them is still too great.'

'Can we pick up what they say? Discover if they know each other.'

'Yes, yes, I suppose so,' Medway was vague in his manner.

'But surely,' Jonas insisted, 'it will be of enormous value.'

'Hm.' His senior rose and looked round at the group. 'I know this is fascinating, but we do have our work, do we not?' Reluctantly the group dispersed. Exit doors closed and the two were left alone.

'Something is wrong?' asked the young scientist.

'No, not wrong. Just, shall we say, puzzling.' The grey-haired man looked round, almost as if to check that they were alone. Then he switched on the screen monitoring the sleeping girl.

'See how uneasily she sleeps. If she were Returning, then by now, in the Neutral Zone, she should be sleeping more calmly. Instead, her excitement is mounting.'

'And that means – wait –,' now the younger man became excited himself. 'It is not a Return, but the start of another Journey?'

'Yes. And it could mean more.'

'How?'

'It could mean that she has abandoned her exploration of that girl's life in 1988, and is travelling deeper into her past ...'

'But that means a change in the experiment – why?'

'I cannot say. And there is another possibility. That she has abandoned her present personality for that of the girl on Screen One and is searching her past for some purpose we cannot work out.'

Jonas leapt from his seat. 'But we can discover what is in her mind surely?'

'We can. But we may still not know why her thoughts run in that direction. We can only watch what she does and hope to find out.'

'But, you seem worried.'

'There is something there which is not right. It is as though – but that's not possible.'

'What?'

"That someone is tampering with the experiment.'

Medway rose and moved across the chamber. 'I think I must speak with the Annexe Director.'

'What, on such vague suspicions?' demanded his colleague. The other turned at the exit and shook his head.

'No, my suspicions I keep to myself for the moment. You too, if you please. But I think he should observe this phase himself.'

He raised his hand to slide back the door, when the young man stopped him with, 'Then you must hurry. The improbability is now an impossibility. There are three in the Neutral Zone.'

6 Roller

At eleven that morning Roller got up from his place in the school hall, and handed his papers to the invigilator. The teacher smiled slightly and shook his head, as if to say 'Finished already' and watched the massively-built lad push through the swing doors.

'There goes someone,' he thought, 'who's got everything and doesn't seem to need any of it.'

Roller was not even thinking of the exams as he left the school. By now he had on the wheels that gave him his nickname (he was baptized Harris McKenzie) and he was swinging slowly and easily in and out of the shopping centre morning crowds and traffic.

One of his 'A' Level maths questions had set him thinking about something else. Everything Roller did made him think about something else. Which was what made life inside his head so interesting for him.

Two parents, he thought, four grandparents, eight great grandparents, sixteen ... now where does that get us? As he rolled for a second time around the shopping precinct fountain, bowing slightly to the amused and the irritated pensioners sunning themselves, he had it worked out. Back to 1770 and his available ancestors out-numbered the population of Jamaica. He must be related to everyone over there and several other countries besides.

But which? Ivory Coast? Benin? Which part of Africa? They reckoned you could tell by a person's face. He ground to a halt in front of the Tesco plate glass window and studied his own reflection, cheekbones, powerful hooked nose. That nose now, maybe he was the 53rd cousin, twice removed, to Sheikh Yamani. But then, if so, why were he, Ma and his sister still living in a re-conditioned council flat twenty floors up overlooking the gasometer? Someone must have blundered.

Someone else was studying his face, from the inside of the supermarket. The checkout girl's eyes suddenly met his.

He bowed. She suddenly switched her gaze and he wheeled away. Girls, women, often stared at him. But fair exchange. He studied them. He liked them. He liked most people. He had to be pushed very, very hard to make him angry. And very few people ever pushed him. Roller was not the sort you pushed – on purpose. Those who didn't like him, whoever they were, left him alone. And that suited him.

The sound of his Walkman faltered in his ear. He tapped the set and the rich tones swelled up again. Music, movement and the inside of my mind, is what I need, he mused as he weaved round the trail of abandoned trolleys on the slope into the car park. He paused to admire a car parked near the exit, then the reserve part of his mind made him look up. A young policeman, mounted on a cycle, helmet thrust back from a young, red face, was watching him. Roller moved on down the pavement.

For some reason, there were more pigs around town today than a farmyard, pigs with walkie-talkies at the intersections, pigs in cruising cars. That either meant someone very important around, or something very naughty just happened. An early evening paper placard caught his eye. *Is Fiona the girl?* He altered it in his mind, *Is Fiona a girl? The* girl? Who for? What about the rest of us?

His tape ran out. Without faltering in his easy cruising, he swung the bag forward under his arm and selected a replacement, the music began again and he went forward.

What to do now? The day was young. The exams were finished. He had run out of regular school routine. No regular job routine lay ahead. Suddenly he had – what – sixty years' unbroken spare time ahead of him. Do something different.

He braked sharply and turned right, down an unfamiliar street.

'You could make something of yourself, Harris' he could hear his father's sad, insistent voice. That was a joke, in a way, for his father had made very little of himself. Over here he had just dwindled away and then one day, very quietly, he had gone back to Kingston, leaving Ma to cope with three small kids – well no, he and Sis had never been small. Even in their teens both of them loomed over their mother. Only elder brother John was small, and that annoyed him. Big brothers ought to be bigger, didn't they?

Ma let her husband go. Her motto was 'Home is where the heart is', and her heart, when not with the family, was in the Pentecostal chapel down the road, with her friends. She kept the family on the straight and narrow, though she always claimed they disobeyed her – all save John that is.

'Ma,' Roller would say, 'anything you want,

I always do just what you want.'

And she would say, 'Yes, son you do, when you want to.'

Sis with her Rasta friends knew where she belonged. 'Why don't you choose?' she would ask him. 'Decide where you belong.' And he would lay his finger on his forehead and reply, 'In here, I belong, inside me.' Sometimes they would argue, sometimes fall out. But he loved her and she loved him. They were so different, but yet the same.

John *was* different. Five years older than both of them, into computers, his own house across the railway and a nice white girl-friend. They were engaged. Engaged? Imagine, to choose someone and never leave them, for fifty, sixty years. Why am I thinking so much about the future and the past?

A shadow caught his eye. He swerved, nearly up-ending the man in uniform on the corner.

'Mind where you're going ...'

'Yes, sah,' sang back Roller. For a split second the policeman looked angry, then he laughed, and Roller was gone.

Roller paused. He was on the canal bridge. He leant on the stone-work, now warmed by the near noon sun. The sluggish, brown water shining dully in the light stretched away, framed between warehouses on one side, and high park wall and trees on the other. Fifty yards down the road a crowd was gathering, there were five, six squad cars.

Stooping, Roller detached the skates, slid them into his shoulder bag and walked down from the bridge on the tow path. As his boots hit the flinty surface of the path, he broke into a run, breathing deeply. Exercise was what he needed. Get the blood circulating.

An hour later he came upon the tree and the rope. He hid his bag and skates under a bush and went for a swing. Music, movement and the inside of my mind.

Three times he swung to and fro, gathering speed. After that the momentum of the swing took over. It went on for a long, long time.

7 Meeting

'Who are you?'

At the third attempt, the words exploded from Fee's mouth, as though the icy cold that paralysed her had melted inside.

'... are you?'

Like a shouted echo of her own, she now heard the boy's voice. They had been yelling at each other, but the words had been soundless, as though they saw each other through a thick glass screen.

And in that same moment, the cold went from her body. His hand poised over her, suddenly thrust down. She flinched.

'What's wrong with you?' The boy grabbed her arm and helped her to stand.

'I'm sorry. I thought ...'

They stood awkwardly, looking each other over. Around them, the white mist still swirled, cutting off every other sound. Beneath their feet was the rough grass. They were still in the scrub land across the canal, thought Fee. But why ...?

Then she became aware again of the boy's face, pale, dark-eyed and the brutal marks of barely healed cuts and bruises. Without thinking she raised a hand to touch his cheek.

'What's hap . . .'

But now he flinched and almost knocked her hand away.

'Sorry,' she whispered. 'But what's wrong with you? Why are you so nervy?'

'Nervy?' he snapped. 'Who's nervy? What about you? I was giving you a hand up and you thought I was going to jump on you.'

'You can hardly blame me for that. You came on me out of this mist, looking . . . ' Then she stopped at the sudden anger in his face.

'I suppose every time you meet a bloke like me you expect to get mugged or something.'

'Oh don't be ridiculous. I don't know what sort of a person you are.'

'No, but you can guess.' His voice suddenly mimicked hers. 'Persons like you always can.'

The two of them stood now within a foot or two of each other. His head barely reached her shoulders. His white bruised angry face was tilted up. A strange thought flashed through Fee's mind. If she bent down and kissed him now, what would he do? And why had she thought that? Until a few moments ago she had never seen him before. But was it a few moments? How long had they been here? She controlled thoughts and feelings.

'Let's not fight,' she urged. 'I don't know you. All I know is that you came over the canal on the rope, like me, didn't you?'

He nodded. 'It was weird. That canal can't be more than fifteen foot wide, but the swing went on for ever. It was dead cold, and when I landed, I felt frozen, you know, paralysed.'

'But we can't be far from the canal, can we, not more than a few yards,' said Fee wonderingly. She pointed. But neither of them seemed to want to move in that direction.

'Right, but why can't we see it?'

'This mist.'

'That's even crazier,' said the lad. 'This mist, where has it come from? Across there, the sun was shining.'

'It could be just a freak pocket,' she began.

'Bloody big pocket if you ask me. It goes on for miles ... ' He stopped and grabbed her arm. 'Look at that. If we can see those buildings over there, why can't we see the canal?'

'Which buildings?' Fee strained her eyes as she followed his pointing finger. 'I can't see any.'

'You being funny?' he said sharply, then

softened his tone. 'Look, I'm not kidding, about half a mile away, over there, low buildings, like, like … an aerodrome.'

'That's impossible,' her tone was decisive, crushing. 'There are no buildings on this land for miles, just waste-land, rubble, ruins.'

'How do you know?'

'Because … ' It was on the tip of her tongue to say, 'because my family owns every square yard of the land, because my family ruined the whole area.'

'Because … I do,' she finished lamely.

'I don't get this. You reckon to know round here. I don't. I've never been out here ever. Who'd want to. It's a dump. So why …?'

The edge of contempt in his tone sparked a sudden question from her.

'So, what are you doing here? Why come over the canal anyway? And why don't you go back that way?'

His pale face suddenly became more pinched, his black eyes glowed.

'That's nothing …' he began, then he changed tack . 'OK. So why don't you go back that way, eh? Why did you come over here … if there's only ruins and rubble?'

Fee took a deep breath, looked him in the eyes and said 'Because I'm running away – like you are. I don't know where I'm going but I'm not going back.'

He shook his head. 'But why should ...?' then he stopped. 'Look. Just not, you said – don't let's fight. So, no more questions like that. Fair enough?'

Impulsively he pushed out his hand. Fee took it. The small hard fingers rested in hers. There was a sudden warmth between them. They exchanged slow smiles.

'Should we go that way, then?' Fee began. But he did not seem to be listening. Instead he was staring past her.

She looked round. Between the two of them and the canal, had appeared, like a phantom, a tall black figure, who stood, arms wide, body rigid and eyes glaring.

8 The Director

'Three!'

The quiet voice at his shoulder made Jonas turn from the instrument panel. He saw a small, lightly built man in grey, with dark features, high cheekbones and calm grey eyes. Without hesitating, he got to his feet. He did not even need the quick glance from his grey-haired colleague Medway, who stood just behind the newcomer, to know, that this was Anwar, Director of Time Annexe.

'Yes, sir. These two boys. They all seem as baffled as …'

'As you, eh?' The Director sounded amused, but he did not smile.

'You are right to be baffled. One Intruder we have had before, but never two.'

'It could be coincidence, sir, the statistical possibilities …'

'I devised this experiment,' said the Director coolly, then turned to address Medway. 'We shall need to find out who they are.'

'We will check the retro-record.'

'That, too. But I mean, find out who they are now.'

'Surely, sir, only Kera is involved in the experiment now?'

'That is what I thought, but ...'

'I don't understand, sir. Who else in the Centre could be involved?'

'I am thinking not only of Insiders, but of Outsiders.'

'That is incredible, sir.'

'What we have here is incredible already. To begin with, that is not Kera returning.'

'But,' Jonas broke in, 'all the signs were.'

Anwar turned his grey eyes on Jonas, but did not seem to resent the interruption.

'Were, but now are not.' He rested his fingers on the instrument panel. Without looking down, he selected one key, then another. The right-hand screen opened. The picture focussed rapidly. In the inner room the girl now slept calmly.

'Kera is not Returning. She is about to go into the past with the – other girl. Why, I cannot yet say. It is not even clear if she knows what is happening. For some reason, of her own free will or not, she is venturing deeper into the unknown.'

'We can reach her, sir, warn her,' urged Medway. 'We have done this before, when there is a danger of people being trapped in their past.'

The Director's mouth tightened.

'Medway, I know as well as you what we have done and what we can do. I will also tell you what we are going to do.'

He paused.

'One Intruder is a coincidence. Perhaps an accident. Perhaps even a fault in the experiment. Two,' his voice rose slightly, 'is a new experiment.'

'Then we ...'

'We open the Time Track and let all three go where they may. Those three young people there, from 1988. They may return to their own time. Or they may go deeper into their own past ...'

'But, sir, the two boys, they have no training, no experience in Time Track. They will not know when, how...'

'That is true. But we cannot keep them in the Neutral Zone for ever. Nor can we impede Kera.'

His voice rose as if he addressed a meeting or conference. 'Whatever happens we shall be richer in our knowledge. Know who you were, understand who you are, decide who you will be. That is our theme, is it not, Medway, Jonas ... ?'

Jonas bit his lip.

'But, the risks to the Volunteer, to Kera?'

Anwar looked curiously at Jonas.

'Volunteers take risks,' he said quietly, 'We must try not to be personal.'

He turned to Medway.

'Open the Track,' he said.

Later that day, Anwar called Medway into his office.

'Our new team member, Jonas. How do you find him?'

Medway pursed his lips.

'Capable.'

Anwar smiled at the shortness of the answer. 'Yet perhaps a little too personally involved over Kera?'

Medway shook his head.

'That is the strange thing. I don't think he knows her at all. He comes here on the personal say so of the Controller, yet he behaves as though there is no connection. I'm not happy.'

Anwar frowned and tapped his desk.

'Sometimes I think you are over-cautious, over-suspicious of people, Arnold.'

'If you don't mind my saying so, Director, sometimes I think you are too easy going. Why was Kellett transferred to Psy-Vid?'

The Director shrugged.

'He wanted to go. His heart was not in our work.'

'But why the transfer just before our experiment started? And why was this – why was Jonas – sent here, on the Controller's recommendation? I'd never heard of him before.'

Anwar was quiet a moment.

'This won't do, Arnold. Jonas has a good record. One of Carlin's best pupils. You have to give him a chance. You read too much into what could be coincidence.'

Medway answered. 'Coincidences, in life and on Time Track need to be looked at carefully. I intend to make sure nothing, and nobody, harms our project.'

He turned and walked out. Anwar watched him go, thoughtfully.

9 The Neutral Zone

'Pardon me, if I'm interrupting something.'

The words came slowly and with effort from the tall, black boy's mouth. Slowly his body relaxed, a wide smiled parted his face, and he took a careful step forward.

Fee and Tod, embarrassed to find they were still holding hands, let go of each other and turned to the new arrival.

'Don't tell us,' said Fee. 'You went for a walk along the canal. You went for a swing on a rope. It went on forever and now you're in a fog.'

'First you couldn't talk, you couldn't move,' added Tod.

'Don't spoil my story,' grinned the black lad. 'But what are you people doing here?'

'Yeah, well now you're here,' said the slightly built lad, with a quick glance at the girl, 'you might as well know, there are rules.'

'Already?'

'Like, no questions, like why, where from,

for what, and so on.'

'Relax, friend. I was just making conversation. But don't I even get to find out what you people are called. My name's Roller. At least, that's what they call me.'

He looked down at his feet. 'My skates are over the water.'

'My name's Tod.'

'That figures,' answered Roller. 'And the lady?'

'I'm called Fee.'

Roller grinned. 'For Fiona.' A newspaper headline flashed across his mind.

'That's right.' Roller's eyes met the girl's for a moment.

'I thought I'd ...'

'Whatever you thought, mate, forget it,' interrupted Tod. 'We've agreed.'

Roller shrugged. 'Listen. You people have secrets. You keep 'em. I'm not going to stick around where I'm not wanted.'

'Where are you going?'

'Back on that rope.'

'If you can find it. We're going this way,' Tod pointed.

'Nothing that way, but bushes and that old bunch of buildings,' answered Roller.

Tod turned in triumph to Fee. 'See! What

did I tell you, there are buildings over there.'

Fee shook her head vigorously. 'Look, I know it sounds stupid, but I see no building over there. What is more I know there's no building over there. I know this ...'

'That is weird,' said Roller. 'This whole set up is weird. This mist, out of nowhere. This feeling paralysed. Not being able to speak.'

Tod jerked his head towards the mist-covered waste-land. 'I've just thought – if those buildings are one of those secret research places, if this mist were one of those new nerve gases ...'

'Then, why aren't we paralysed any more, man?' demanded Roller. 'Anyway,' he went on, 'if that's the cause, then you people ought to come back this way, over the rope.'

Tod and Fee glanced at one another and shook their heads.

'OK, folks, please yourself. I'm going. This place is creepy anyway.' Roller moved away from them abruptly, and in seconds his tall figure vanished into the mist. Fee looked at Tod.

'Pity about that,' she said, 'he might have been good company.'

'What we need, is not company,' returned Tod. 'We need to get going – over there.'

'What, to that Secret Research Establishment?'

'You taking the mickey – Fee?' he hesitated before using her name.

'Sorry, Tod,' she smiled. 'Anyway, let's go. But go carefully. The ground round here is treacherous. There are hidden hollows and shafts, which haven't all been sealed off.'

'You do know about this place, don't you?'

'Look, forget it, will you.' She strode away into the mist and Tod had to hurry to catch up with her. The ground was broken and uneven, pitted with holes, lumpy with concealed boulders and crumbling brickwork. Bushes and brambles caught jaggedly at their clothing and slowed them down. For a good half hour they toiled on. But the buildings seemed to come no nearer to them. In places the way dipped sharply into hollows where the mist seemed to lie more thickly and all sight of the buildings were lost.

Coming out of one hollow they lost sight of one another, searching in growing panic they shouted each others names, ran here and there, tripped and stumbled then finally crashed heavily against one another and rolled on the ground.

As Fee pulled Tod to his feet, she looked with concern at his bruised face.

'Are you OK, Tod? Do you want to rest?'

They were on level ground again now and the grass was less broken by debris. Tod grinned and shook his head.

'Funny thing is Fee. I don't feel anything now. It all seems right in the past. As if it hadn't happened.'

'Right, Tod. That's how I feel. As though everything that's happened to me before we came here doesn't matter any more. As though everything started when I saw you, and the other boy …'

'Oh, Roller, you mean. Well, he'll be back on his skates now, on his way into town, having his Kentucky Fried …'

'And I do not even like chicken.'

The now familiar voice spoke out of the mist.

Tod and Fee stopped and stared. There, only a few paces in front of them, stood the tall figure of Roller.

'What happened? Did you change your mind?'

'No, I just did not find the rope.'

'What?'

'No way.'

'So you followed us, eh?'

'Uh uh', Roller shook his head. 'You followed me.'

'What's that supposed to mean?'

'What it says. I've not moved more than twenty yards in a circle round here from where we all landed. When I found no canal, I made up my mind it was no good struggling through the briars and messing myself up. So I sat and waited.'

'But this is ridiculous,' said Fee. 'We've been going for the best part of an hour.'

'That's right, in a big circle. I've been going in a small one.'

'Look,' went on Roller. 'Did you get anywhere nearer that building?'

'No,' answered Fee, 'but then, I didn't expect to. The building doesn't exist.'

'Maybe you didn't expect to. But Tod, there, did.'

Tod nodded. 'Too right. But it seemed to go further away all the time – like – a mirage.'

'Right,' said Roller, 'and if you walked that way, for hours, you wouldn't get to any canal, either.'

'But that's stupid. It's got to be there. It was where we came over.'

'Yes, course it was,' agreed Roller. 'But is it *now*?'

'This fog's got into your brain.'

'At least my brain does not come up with

non-existent War Research Establishments and paralysing nerve gases floating about on one side of a canal and not the other.'

'But the buildings are there. You saw 'em even if Fee didn't.'

'Sure. But no matter how hard you walked you never got there.' Roller sat down and waved to the other two to join him. After a moment's silence, he said, 'I've been thinking. Now don't be sarky. When we rode that rope, the swing went on forever. But we were still just across the canal. We landed. We saw each other, but we couldn't talk. Light first, sound after. Like lightning then thunder. The difference is time.'

'Great stuff, mate. Time travel you mean. Pull the other.'

'Don't be so quick, Tod,' broke in Fee. 'Unless we are all dreaming, why can't we get anywhere?'

'All right,' retorted Tod. 'If we time travelled, you first, then me, why did we all catch up with one another, Roller, eh?'

Roller shook his head. 'Man, I don't know. Unless this area's some kind of dead zone. You know where there's no time. So there's no space either. You get nowhere. You get nowhen.'

He grabbed for Fee's wrist.

'Look!'

Fee pulled back her hand and looked at her watch.

'It's stopped. At 6.30 when I came across the canal.'

'You could have knocked it,' said Tod.

'I know what I'm saying's fantastic,' went on Roller, 'but as old Sherlock remarked ...'

'Eh,' said Tod.

'Yes,' put in Fee. 'Eliminate all other possibilities. What's left, however incredible, has to be the truth.'

'Oh, clever stuff,' said Tod sourly, glaring at the other two.

'Relax, friend. No wonder your name's Tod. You are so-o prickly.'

Tod jerked up. 'Look, mate.'

Fee put her arm across his shoulder.

'Relax, Tod. Roller is right. Wherever we are, whenever we are, we are stuck with each other. As if we were on a desert island. We cannot afford to quarrel.'

Tod pulled a face. 'OK. But what do we do?'

Roller uncoiled his legs and stretched out full length in the grass.

'What can you do with time but let it pass?'

'He's right,' said Fee. She stretched out in the grass not far away from the black lad. Tod noticed how the two were as tall as one another.

And, he observed grudgingly, just as good looking, and as smart. For a moment he felt excluded – a familiar feeling of dark depression came over him. Desperately he wanted to talk, to tell someone what had happened to him last night. But …

Fee was sitting up, staring at him.

'What did you say?' she demanded.

'Me? Nothing.'

'But you did. You spoke. Someone spoke. Was it Roller?'

'It was not Roller,' replied the black lad, opening his eyes. 'Mr Roller, if you please, Madame, was asleep. Very comfortably asleep.'

'Well I was not, and I heard someone talk. Men's voices. Two or three of them. As though there was a conversation going on in the next room.'

'Hey this is getting heavy, Fee,' said Roller sitting up and putting a hand on her arm. 'This place is getting to you.'

'Don't you patronise me.' Tod stared at the haughty anger in Fee's voice. 'You two saw buildings that I didn't. Did I say you were out of your mind? People were talking.'

'What did they say?' Tod asked. 'Can you remember?'

'At first it was just odd words, snatches,

words like "track", "experiment", "coincidence", "intruder". It was funny – like doctors discussing a patient who they think can't hear them. Talking about "her". Then someone, who seemed to be in charge, spoke quite clearly, as though he were laying down the law. Funny his voice was so familiar to me.'

'What did he say?' demanded Roller, eagerly.

'Know who you were …' she paused. 'Know who you are – no, that wasn't it … it was … Know who you were. Understand who you are. Decide what you will be.'

'Hey that makes sense!'

'Thank *you*, Roller.'

'No fun. That does make sense. Know who you were, that's past. Understand who you are, that's present. Decide what you will be, that's future. It's time.'

'But it doesn't make sense, mate. I know who I've been all my life.' Tod's voice was suddenly aggressive.

'Yeah, but who were you before that – father, grandfather, even further back … everybody who's gone before. You don't know them. If you did, imagine …'

For a moment, all three were deep in thought. Know who you were. Tod and Fee exchanged glances.

Roller was on his feet now, waving his arms.

'That is what that rope is for. To travel through time, to find out just who you were.'

Raising his hands above his head he shouted. 'What are you waiting for *Mister*? Open up the time and let us through. Let it swing.'

'Look,' gasped Fee.

About them the mist was paling, parting, as if blown by a wind. First blue sky, then sun came back into view. A yard or two from them, rising out of the grass, towered the gnarled trunk of the old oak tree. And from its branches swinging gently towards them hung the rope.

'Let's go,' shouted Roller. 'Who's first?'

10 Time Swing

One by one they took the rope and launched into the air. Around them trees, water, sky blended. Colour and shape melted and they swooped through a cold pale world of silence.

Fear then wild excitement came as the boundless downward swing accelerated beyond all speed they could know or imagine.

In the great, deep curve of the time swing, shape and colour returned as a thousand pictures, like a crazily speeded-up film, shot through their minds.

First came scenes and faces that they recognised, or half recognised, like friends spotted from a hurtling train, then more figures, faces unknown, now clear, now blurred.

And, with the shapes and features came the shock of feeling, living pain and pleasure, heat of love and hate, laughter echoing in their skulls, tears flooding their cheeks.

They grew, they shrank, strength came and weakness; over and over again it happened.

Until, for each of them came the giant, upward curve, speed slowing, excitement dying and the frantic flurry of images fading away.

And the curve moved at last into darkness, as for Fee, Roller and Tod the Time Rope swing died.

What and how it stopped they could not say. Though they had each one chosen where to leave their travelling, chosen even without realising it.

And having chosen, their past life took them in. They lived it now, forgetting what their future was.

11 Fee

Meg stirred, then woke. The room was dark but a tiny gap in the heavy curtains showed grey light. Thrusting back the covers she swung lightly to the floor and tiptoed to the window. Raising the curtain she saw out across parkland and woods to the moors beyond. It would be fine today.

Light from the window fell on a couch. Over the back was spread a fine blue gown awash with lace and ribbons. It suited her well. They all said so yesterday. And after five times on and off, and much tucking and stitching, it fitted her like a glove.

She turned her back on it and let the curtain fall. Quickly she drew off the night gown and threw it on to the bed. Naked she strode to the closet door, opened it and pulled out a wicker basket. From it she took out a coarse smock which she put on. Tying an old green bonnet under her chin, she took up the basket in one hand, a pair of wooden clogs in the other and left the room.

Lightly, barefooted she walked down the passages, carefully opened the farthest door and went into the gallery. She exchanged glances with her ancestors as they looked down from their frames on the wall. Today she was due to join them. Hence the blue dress. At two o'clock, the portrait painter hired from Amsterdam, would come for a first sitting. And at four, George Peverell, her intended, would follow. This morning, though, she was still her own mistress.

As she took on her clogs and walked across the stable yard, a maid and young groom watched her go.

'Imagine,' said the maid, 'to have that blue gown worth two year's wages, and then to go out like a farm girl.'

'Mr Peverell'll put a stop to that when they wed,' she added.

'Now that's a thing. Why's Lady Margaret marrying him? He's nobody in this county,' asked the groom.

'For one,' answered the maid, 'he's nobody, but he's not nothing. He could buy and sell Hordens ten times over. Iron, coal. He's a finger in every pie. What he ain't got is land and title. Hordens have both.'

'And, for another,' put in the groom. 'If

Lord Horden says she'll marry him, she will, eh?'

'True, though she's a will of her own.'

'I've heard say she's a bit ...' the groom tapped his head.

'Oh, you have, have you,' snapped the maid. 'Well, she's got more in her head than anyone round here, Vicar and all.'

While they talked, Meg had crossed the park. She left the path, cut across the grass and clambered over the farther wall, balancing neatly on the crumbling stone. By the time Lord Horden had breakfasted and was demanding testily where Lady Margaret might be, Meg was leaving the tree line for the open slopes, clambering among boulders, scrambling across patches of scree, bonnet loose, brown face damp with sweat.

As she climbed, she paused here and there, picking up a pebble, or breaking off a fragment of rock with a small hammer she took from her basket. Sometimes she turned aside, to take up flowers and roots, stowing them carefully away in gathered moss. All morning she worked, eating brown bread from her pockets, drinking when thirsty from rock pools. Absorbed in her work, enjoying the fresh moor air and the freedom, she paid no heed to time. Then she saw her shadow lengthening on the heather before her.

She shrugged. The portrait painter would now be waiting. Well he could wait. Her face would be there tomorrow. But, now, Mr Peverell, that was another matter. Things were cool enough between her and her father without a snub to the intended. Besides, Mr Peverell had given her no cause for offence – yet. She'd never met him. And she had a life time to get to know him. She'd go back now, though he'd need to wait a while for her to change.

Deep in thought, she came down the slope off the moorland, and into the new plantation of trees her father had had planted. They were to stand between The Hall and the course of the new canal that was to carry Peverell coal and iron to the sea. That would make Hordens wealthy again. But there was no need to look on the grime and ugliness that brought the money.

Other things would be concealed once she was married. Peverell would change his name. The natural order would be reversed. By magic he would become a Horden. In two generations who would know the difference? And she would make it all happen just by doing as she was asked. Did she care, she wondered? It depended, perhaps on whether Peverell let her lead her own life. If he left her free to roam the moors and pore over the roots and rocks in her small back room behind the gallery then things might go well. But no one would force her …

In that moment a shadow rose up in front of her. She was roughly grabbed, and an unshaven face was thrust into hers. Breath reeking of spirits was blown into her mouth. Her basket flew from her hands as she struck out and struggled to come free.

'Eh, lads. A fighter!'

Around her were half a dozen muscular, work stained men, open-shirted, coloured neck-ties at their throats.

'Let me go,' she commanded. For a second the force of her voice made the grip slacken. She tore free.

'Fancies herself, too.' Her attacker looked round at his companions who seemed to hesitate. A look of fury came into his eyes. Snatching her again, he lifted her off her feet.

'Now you'll see what happens to girls who fancy 'emselves,' he grunted. Turning to the others he said, 'Shove off. I'll have this one to myself.'

Meg felt herself dragged through bushes that tore at her smock, then thrown heavily to the grass.

12 Fee

'Let the girl go, Marker.'

The voice was quiet, but deep. While her attacker swayed over her, Meg rolled to one side and scrambled to her feet. A yard or two away stood three other men, canal workers, dirty and clay stained. The one who spoke was tall, dark-haired, his young face reddened with the weather.

'Lay off, Maguire,' snarled Marker. 'Just because you're the spokesman don't give you the right to interfere with my private business.'

'Ah but your private business don't suit her, Marker. So, on your way or ...'

'Or?'

'Or I'll smash your ugly whiskey sodden mouth.'

For a moment the two men eyed each other, then Marker changed his mind and pushing past Meg blundered off into the trees.

Maguire turned to the others. 'Go after him, lads, and tell him if he don't leave the site by tomorrow, we'll run him off.'

'I'm sorry, Miss,' he had turned to Meg. 'Look, I've got your basket, but some of your flowers and stones have gone.'

'Thank you – Mr Maguire,' Meg tried to straighten her bonnet, but gave up and snatched the strings from her neck. She took the basket from him and began to arrange the contents.

'I'll walk back with you to the village, Miss ...'

'Meg, Meg Harland,' Meg quickly lied. 'There's no need. I must hurry. I'm late.'

'I will walk with you to the road, still,' he insisted. 'You shall not go home and say we navigators are a lot of savages, just for one drunk.'

'Why should I say, that?'

'All the people in the town say that. They say that in every part where we dig. But they don't mind if we do their dirty work for them.'

They had left the plantation now and were walking a cow path that led down to the farms on the village outskirts. Meg looked sideways at him.

'Prejudice is a bad thing, Mr Maguire. So you should not guess at what I think.'

He turned and smiled wryly. 'I beg your pardon. See, I'll make amends for that and for the insult you've just suffered.' From his pocket he took out two flat stones. Meg gasped. Inset in each, like a painter's handiwork, were the delicate shapes of ferns. She had seen these before in other collections.

'Where did you come by those, Mr Maguire?'

'In the cutting, Miss Harland. We often find them when we go deep down.'

'Will you show me where you found them?' she asked eagerly.

'It's two miles west of here. Perhaps.'

They were now walking on the village street. People in cottage doorways eyed them. Meg bit her lip.

'Mr Maguire. You have been kind. I must now leave you.'

He took off his cap.

'My pleasure.'

'See, Mr Maguire. If tomorrow in the afternoon, I were to be on the hill above the plantation, might you spare an hour to show me the cutting where these fossils were found?'

He turned red, then walked abruptly away.

An hour later, Meg, in the blue gown, took her place at table. Her father Lord Horden, lean, hook nosed, long-armed, the Vicar, plump, his beady eyes darting here and there, and a powerful, broad-shouldered, black-browed man, crop-haired but wigless, were waiting for her.

Her father, for once, was in good humour, making light of being kept waiting. The vicar was full of compliments about her dress. The other man, George Peverell greeted her courteously. She guessed that fashionable manners came hard to him, though. Those sharp eyes were more concerned with other things.

Over dinner the conversation turned rapidly to the canal workings and her father questioned Peverell eagerly about how long the task would take. Not more than two months more, Peverell assured him, before the canal cut reached the river.

'That's good news, Peverell,' said Lord Horden.

'Yes,' said the vicar smoothly, 'and it will be good news for our townsfolk and their families.'

'How so?'

'Then the barbarians you, sir, are obliged to employ to dig the canal can take themselves away and leave us in peace.'

'Barbarians are good enough to make money for us, but not to mix with us, then?' demanded Meg. She saw Peverell's eyebrow raise. He changed the tack of the conversation.

'We shall be finished sooner, but for some trouble.'

'What trouble?' asked Lord Horden.

'The Irish among the navigators have found a spokesman called Maguire, a man of ability put to bad use. They've demanded sixpence a day more for hard going. What's worse, the English are inclined to follow him as well. If he were not there, the work would go faster.'

Again he looked curiously at Meg. Her cheeks warmed and she looked at her plate.

'Lady Margaret. I must congratulate you, on your findings and discoveries.'

'I beg your pardon, sir?' Meg's voice was sharp and suspicious. Horden broke in, his voice soothing.

'Ah, Meg. I took the liberty of showing Mr Peverell those rocks of yours. He says they indicate much mineral wealth in our upland acres.'

'I know they do,' retorted Meg, 'but did not expect that…' now she saw Peverell was embarrassed and lowered his head.

The vicar put in a word. 'All my fault Lady Margaret. 'Twas I who told Mr Peverell of your amusements.'

'They are not amusements,' returned Meg.

'They are also, not for public view.'

The awkward silence seemed to hang around the rest of the evening. As soon as she could, Meg excused herself and left the men.

That next morning dawned cool and cloudy. By eleven the rain was pouring down. Reluctantly Meg agreed to sit for the portrait painter, who tried in vain to make her smile. He shrugged and said, 'It will be terrible. And that will be a pity.'

Suddenly Meg laughed at the thought and the Dutchman snatched up his pencil again. For an hour he worked away, then a shaft of sunlight struck through a window. Meg leapt to her feet and rushed from the room, ignoring his protests.

Quickly changing into her smock, snatching up her basket, she left The Hall and walking and running, climbing and scrambling, she reached the crest of the first moorland slopes by early afternoon. The land was empty save for a stooping hawk. She waited another hour. There was no sign of Maguire.

Slowly, disappointed, yet angry with herself for her impulsiveness, she made her way down through the plantation. She took the path close to the canal workings now aswarm with men, trucks, horses. Once or twice she met navvies.

They stood aside and let her pass without a word. But there was no sign of Maguire.

The next day the same happened. In the morning, the portrait painter. At noon a mad dash to get changed and then scrambling up rock and scree to a lonely walk looking moodily at plants and stones, but finding little of interest.

But on the third day towards sunset, she spotted a solitary walker on a lower path. Like a mountain goat she leapt from hump to hump and rock to rock and slithered finally feet first on to the track to confront him. Maguire stood still, his face red with embarrassment, as she greeted him, smoothing down the torn and dirtied back of her smock.

'Why did you not meet me?' the words burst out.

He looked away, 'I thought best not.'

'You thought best not. That was unfriendly, Mr Maguire, and from someone who had shown me kindness.'

'I did not know,' he stammered, then suddenly, he was angry. 'You did not tell me your true name ... Lady Horden. That was unfriendly, to pretend. Am I not good enough to ...'

'Oh, don't be ... how did you discover?' She

made way for him and walked at his side.

'Why, your vicar stopped me, near the village.'

'That scoundrel!' At the anger in her voice, Maguire turned and grinned, then was suddenly serious.

'He told me you were betrothed to Mr Peverell, our employer. I thought it best to ...'

'So, the great spokesman John Maguire is afraid of something is he?'

He flushed. 'That was unkind. I thought of your reputation. People will say evil things even if people walk and talk together.'

She stopped and put a hand on his arm.

'I beg your pardon. I have done you wrong, twice. Once not to tell you my name, once to make you a coward when I know you are not. But John Maguire. Neither am I a coward or a slave. I will walk with whom I please, betrothed or not – and I am not yet.'

He looked away. 'These past three days I've watched you walk on the moors. I've been quite near you, when you didn't see, just to be sure you came to no harm.'

Now she looked away. Gathering her courage, she said, 'Now will you please walk with me to the place you told me of. We will talk. I'll call you John, you call me Meg and that will be enough.'

'That will be my pleasure – Meg.'

So that day, and other days, they walked together. They made their meetings on the high moor in the early morning and before sunset. In the hours between, Meg sat for the portrait painter and now and then met Peverell at dinner. The portrait painter was happy. 'This will be wonderful. You smile all the time.'

Weeks passed. The mighty cutting carved by the muscles of the navvies marched towards the river. One late afternoon Maguire told Meg, 'In ten day's time, we'll be away.'

'No!' the word burst from her.

He put his hands on her shoulders. 'If you were Meg Harland, I would say ...'

'What would you say?'

'Come with me and we'll take ship to Van Dieman's land where no one knows or cares what name you have.'

She pulled away from him and ran as fast as she could down the hill track. For two days she did not dare go to the moors. And then something happened that changed her mood. As she came out of church that Sunday, the vicar came up close to her and whispered in his oily way, 'Take care Lady Margaret what company you keep.'

She ignored him and hurried away. That afternoon she took her blue gown and with a knife slit up the hems so that she could walk freely in it. Then she set off in the warm light of the setting sun, up the path to the moors. On the highest point she met John Maguire. They kissed in silence.

Then she drew him down to a grassy hollow in the rocks. They lay together on the short turf, their bodies warm together. He kissed her again, slowly and shyly until she grew impatient with his shyness, pushed him a little aside, dragged up the skirts until the breeze blew coolly on her hips and waist. He struggled with his clothes. She saw the freed flesh spring up, then closed her eyes and drew him to her.

13 Roller

Kwame lay under the forest night and watched the moon ride high above the dark tangle of branches. From time to time he raised his shackled wrists and carefully rubbed the raw, sore muscles of his neck and throat. The wooden yoke which tied him to the next man in line as they marched through the day, was taken off at night. The guards knew that arm and leg chains were enough to keep the weary, travel-sick slaves from any wild attempt to run away. They sat, drank and joked around their fire fifty yards away, barely bothering to watch whether their prisoners, seventy men, women and children, woke or slept, moved or kept still.

Four months ago the slavers had raided Kwame's village on the coast, taking many captive, stowing them in the stinking, disease-ridden barracoons together with other people from places inland. The inland people were paralysed with dread when they saw the ocean with its great, white-capped waves, this great green waste of water that stretched away to the far horizon. Kwame's people were sea-fishers and had no fear of the Atlantic. It brought them their food. They rode on its waves with confidence and excitement.

But the voyage they made was unlike any they had known. Taken on board the slavers' sailing ship, they were pushed into the dark hold, chained to the timbers heaving with the rise and fall of the sea outside, fed once a day a foul mess of beans, and left to endure and survive as best they could, while the ship sailed on to the West.

Days and weeks passed. One by one, the weaker slaves sickened and died. And as they died the sailors came down from above, pulled up the corpses and hurled them into the sea. The inland folk sickened first. Fear and desperation made them easy victims to disease. But soon the death and sickness came to Kwame's people, too. Old ones, children, babies born on the voyage, they were taken and thrown overboard.

Kwame had one hope. Not for himself. That hope had gone on the day he had last seen the yellow beach and green forests of his home. But among the village folk taken by the slavers was Nkansa, his love. And inside Nkansa's body was their child. One day, at sea, when they had been briefly allowed up on deck to exercise, he had seen her, down the line, among the other women and children. She had looked at him, a long steady glance, and had gently passed her hand over the curve of her own stomach, to tell him that, so far, their child was safe.

Even slavers are not safe. Half way across the ocean, disease struck the crew – those men who dragged the dead and dying from the hold were first to go down. And in the crew's quarters, the sickness spread. Several died, and soon the captain grew anxious. He feared that the ship might not make the end of the voyage.

And if she sank in foul weather, the crew might take to the boats and leave the slaves to die with the ship. But then all the profit of the voyage would be lost, and he would never be employed again by the merchants who traded in human flesh.

So, as the weather worsened and blew into a storm, he did a desperate thing. He set free Kwame and some of his mates from their chains below and had them brought up on deck, to help sail the ship. Half dazed and stiff from their shackles, weakened by rotten food, at first they staggered on the deck like drunks. But before long they got back their strength, sprang in the rigging and worked with the crew to bring the vessel back on course.

'We are fools,' muttered one of Kwame's friends to him as they hauled on ropes and grappled with the tattered wind-torn sails. 'They get us to save this ship and their lives. Then they land us on the other shore and sell us like cattle.'

But Kwame shook his head.

'If this ship goes down, then all our people go down with it. What chance will they stand, chained to the beams?'

In his mind he saw Nkansa and the other women, and the children, choking and dying, drowning as the waters burst into the hold and the ship dragged them down. So he worked on rope and canvas like a demon.

When the storm had passed and the ship sailed into calmer water, the bosun told Kwame. 'You're a good sailor. See. I'll buy you from the captain. Then you ship with me. And you can pay me back as you earn your wages. In two trips like this, you'll be a free man.'

Kwame, when he understood what was being offered hin – to get his freedom by shipping his own people into slavery, at first was tempted to spit in the man's face. But held back. One such act could get him flogged until the blood ran down his back.

And he answered cunningly. 'You buy Nkansa and me, and I'll work to pay you back.'

'Huh,' snorted the mate. 'I'm not in business for families. You and you only. That's my offer. Take it or leave it.' He laughed. 'What's your worry? You can get another woman any time in any port.'

Another woman. Leave Nkansa and their child to be sold away on the other shore, while he bought his own freedom. He shook his head.

'Suit yourself,' said the bosun. 'Get below.'

Kwame went below and joined his people, while the ship taking them into slavery sailed on. But there was now one difference. While he worked on deck, when no one watched, Kwame had stolen a broken file, a slice of metal not more than three inches long. He hid it, first in his clothing, then in his hair, sometimes in his clenched fist, sometimes trapped between body and arm. He hid it and made his plan.

14 Roller

When the ship's human cargo was landed in Jamaica to be sold to the plantation owners, there were no more than thirty of Kwame's people left, men women and children. And they were sold, together with forty of the inland folk in one lot to the owner of a large plantation some four days' march away in the hills. His agent paid extra for Nkansa. For it was clear she now carried a child. And she was a strong, handsome girl.

Kwame watched from the crowd of chained slaves as she was stood up on the auction block and the plantation agents walked around her, fingered her flesh and exchanged grins and remarks. A hot rage came sweeping up inside him, filling his head. Even his leg irons would not have stopped him rushing, stumbling out to attack them, if older men around him had not held him back, and whispered caution to him. They had learnt much since they were taken from their homes across the ocean. They were men with pride and they had learnt how to be humble, how to hide their real feelings. They now knew what it was to be treated like animals and to keep their human thoughts and emotions locked inside them.

Next day, at dawn, the slave column set out marching north-westwards away from the flat land near the port and up into the hills, through which they would have to pass to reach their new owner's land. Rich as he was, he was set on becoming richer. He intended to clear more forest and scrub land, plant more sugar cane. He needed more slaves and had sent ten heavily armed men to guard them on the four day march. They travelled slowly, the slaves were still weak from the voyage below decks.

The guards were in no hurry. They had been ordered not to push the slaves too hard. Their strength would be needed for future days. So they marched slowly. If a slave, unused to walking on rough ground with legs chained together, neck clamped into a wooden yoke, stumbled and fell, the guards would lazily prod and kick him till he rose and stumbled on.

At night, the women and the children were taken from the line, released and set apart, the youngest tied lightly with rope, the mothers feeding children left quite free. The guards guessed that now the journey's end was near, the will to resist, to escape, to run away into unknown mountain forests in a strange far off land, would be low.

Kwame watched and studied all these things as they marched, as the route took them higher among the hills and rocks, as the trees and bushes gradually thinned out and the column moved more slowly, halted more often.

At night, when others slept, he stayed awake, until an hour or two before dawn. He was young and strong enough to live a while on a few hours sleep. He had a better way to spend his time than sleeping. With patient care, and keeping one eye always on the guards by their fire or roving now and then along the sleeping line of slaves, Kwame began to use his tiny, broken file, to saw into the heavy metal of his leg chain.

It was slow and painful work. He lay on his back, one leg doubled under him, slowly sawing at the point where the chain link joined the metal clamp around his ankles. Unable to see in the dark, unwilling to attract attention by sitting up, he pretended to sleep, while his fingers guided the file as it bit into the metal fraction by fraction. Now and again the file edge trapped his skin. He felt the blood run and bit his teeth, so as not to cry out. He lay and watched the moon and as the moments passed in the hot night he worked and worked to cut the iron that held him.

His plan was simple. When the links on either end of the chain were nearly severed and the time was right, he would crawl down the line to where the women and children slept. There he would wake Nkansa, cut her rope and together they would steal away into the forest. Once at a safe distance, he would finally break his chain on a rock and they would run. Where they would run, he did not know. Perhaps to the coast and the shore. They would know how to live there. He knew. He had heard on the voyage, stories of slaves who had escaped. There were other stories too. He had heard those. Of slaves hunted with dogs and torn to pieces before the hunters could call the hounds off, of slaves whose feet were broken with axe blades to cripple them – not enough to stop them working but enough to stop them running. Slaves had been flogged until they died, hanged and burned alive. But he would not die, Nkansa would not die, their child would not die, because they would not be caught.

By dawn he took earth from beneath his body and rubbed on the raw metal edge he had filed and dragged himself up with the others to begin their slow, exhausted march up the next hill slope. They were halfway there now, and deep into the mountain country.

That night came near disaster. Instead of drinking by their fire, the guards roamed nervously up and down, checking and counting the slaves. One guard came close to Kwame, turning over sleeping slaves, inspecting their chains. He had barely time to stab the file into the earth as the lantern beam swept over his body. His eyes met the guard's for a moment above the glare. He felt a violent shock to his side as the man's boot thudded into him. He dropped his head and eyes. The guard passed on. But the excitement did not cease. The escort stayed awake, gathering uneasily together in the light of their lamps, muttering to each other. Over and over he heard the word 'Maroon', 'Maroon.'

Next day as the column began to get under way, the slaves were whispering the word. Someone knew, how no one knew, that somewhere in the hills above them among the trees and bushes men were lurking, armed men. They were slaves who had escaped and could not be brought to heel. They were called Cimaroons, an old Spanish word. But here they called them Maroons. And the guards feared them more than any other thing. They dreaded the silent ambush in the night hours that might leave them with their throats cut. For the Maroons gave no quarter to their enemies.

The story filled Kwame's heart with fierce joy. That night he put all caution aside, and when his fellow slaves had barely fallen asleep and the guards still roved about moving between two fires they had lit at head and rear of the column, Kwame sat up and heedless of the grating squeal of metal on metal, sawed away at the last thin link of chain by his left ankle. Two minutes of frenzied cutting ended in a wild jerk as the iron snapped. Without looking up or round he began to hack away madly at the half-snapped iron on his right leg.

The darkness round him suddenly lit up.

'Look at this bastard!'

The yell from the guard who stood over Kwame, lantern in hand, set the column in uproar. An inch away from his upturned face he saw the muzzle of the guard's musket. And in the light of the lamp, he saw the trigger finger tighten.

15 Tod

The little valley was a lovely place, but strange to the young pale-faced Britons who lay among the rocks of the ridge above. The brown earth, the gnarled olive trees, the golden green of orange trees in the groves below, and overhead the startling blue sky and burning sun.

Stranger still were the great scars and gashes in the earth, the smashed trees, the ruins of white walled houses with smoke still rising from them into the still air. For this was a peaceful land at war – civil war. This was Spain 1937. The young Britons, students and factory workers, were part of the Republican front line that ran along the ridge. Across the valley in the hills a half mile away were the crack troops of General Franco's fascist forces. And overhead, like silver sharks in a blue sea, cruised the planes which Hitler had sent from Germany to help his ally.

This company of the International Brigade, two days ago, had forced a crossing of the river and driven the fascists from the ridge. But they had paid the price in many killed and wounded. Fresh volunteers had been rushed from Barcelona to take their place. Weary from travel in rattling trucks over dusty roads, dizzy from the heat, shoulders still sore from training with rifles they handled for the first time just a fortnight ago, they now waited, and thought of home, and began to wonder if it was fear that was at work in their insides.

Above them, near the crest of the ridge, back against a tree stood a group of officers. One or two in the uniforms of regular soldiers, others in the rough uniforms of the rank and file, others in green jackets and pants. One of these, who carried no weapons, was speaking. His voice floated away in the empty air, barely reaching the recruits who lay at the farther edge of the hollow. He was telling them about the military and political situation, what the German Nazis were doing, what the British Government was not doing, what the Soviet Union was doing. He used long words. Some of his audience heard him with great attention, others barely understood his drift, others were half asleep in the heat. They wanted him to finish so that they could roll further into the shade.

At last he stood down. An awkward silence fell, before one of the officers began a polite clapping, picked up by some of the audience. Quickly another officer moved forward to give the order to dismiss, when he was interrupted.

'Comrade!'

From the shade of a tree, behind the recruits, where sat a group of more seasoned Brigaders, rose a small figure in uniform, thin, wiry, face deep brown from the Spanish sun.

'Yes?' said the officer uncertainly.

'Can I say something?' There was a touch of the Londoner in his voice.

Almost without waiting for permission, he pushed down into the middle of the hollow and spoke directly to the new men.

'Look – comrades. I know what you're thinking. I know what you're feeling. You've been on the road a long time. You feel a bit sick inside and it's not just the food.'

A nervous laugh escaped the audience. Some of the officers smiled.

'Some of you left home because you're brassed off with being on the dole. Some of you wanted adventure. All of you want to help the Spanish people. Some of you came in the holds of bloody coffin ships. Some of you sneaked across the border to avoid the French police. You've come a long way and you've never seen a shot fired in anger outside a fairground.

'Some of you are going to get killed ...'

One of the officers stepped forward as if to interrupt, but another held him back. The little soldier went on.

'Some of you are going to get crippled. Some of you'll get back home safely to tell your kids and your grandchildren if you're lucky. Some of you'll wind up in the pox hospital if I'm any judge of human nature.'

A gust of laughter swept the audience. Some of the recruits sat up.

'But let me tell you something. You're like me. Why did I come here, if I didn't want my head seeing to? I worked in the docks. They treated us like rats. Fighting. Fighting's nothing to us, is it? We fought for a bleeding living.

'And then Mosley and the blackshirts started marching in the East End, beating up the Jews. And I thought what do I care about Jews? And the answer I came up with was this. If you let 'em beat up Jews today, they'll come and do it to you tomorrow. Tomorrow it'll be Reds, or pinks, or people with two left feet.'

He paused. The silence now had an edge as everyone waited for his next word.

'And if you let Franco and Hitler beat up – ' he pointed upwards. 'See those lovely silver birds up there. The other day they were bombing women and kids. That's the job they do best. If we let Franco and Hitler beat up the Spanish people, sure as night follows day, they'll beat us up tomorrow. And tomorrow's too late.

'I'll tell you one thing more. Blokes like you pushed the fascists off this ridge. Before long, you're going to push 'em off those hills and into the sea.'

Abruptly, the speaker pushed his way back into the crowd, which exploded in a great wave of cheering.

The political officer turned to the group around him.

'Who's that comrade?'

One answered, 'George Morris. Came out six months ago.'

'Does he always speak out of turn?'

'Does everything out of turn. Wish we had two thousand like him, we'd turn the bloody world upside down.'

The political officer shrugged.

'He's the sort that could do something rash.'

'True enough. Our George has got it here, in his guts. Whatever he does though – it'll be on the right side.'

'We'll see.'

16 Tod

Next day began with a massive bombardment from big guns across the valley. In the blue air above the white sharks swam into view, turned belly up and dived down to rain high explosives on the narrow trenches carved in the shallow brown earth, where the new volunteers got their first taste of war.

After the bombardment came the assault. First waves of troops brought in from North Africa, that fell on the lower slopes of the ridge and then drew back, leaving the bare rock scattered with bodies. There were dead on the ridge, too, lads of eighteen and men old enough to be their fathers, veterans of this and earlier wars, and boys fresh out from home.

But the line held, though the line grew thin as the day wore on, the heat mounted and the first hint of the stench of death began to fill the air. In the afternoon, the fascist's main forces were thrown in and the human wave lapped dangerously close to the entrenchments on the slopes.

'There's the danger point,' said the battalion commander to his company officers as they lay, binoculars in hand just below the crest of the ridge. 'See where the track comes up from the village, between the trees. Once they get up there into that timber where the rocks begin, they've got cover. Bring the rest of B company up.'

'They came up two hours ago. You want more men, we'll need to pull 'em out from along the line.'

'Can't do that. They know how many we've got. This could be just a feint to get us to thin out too much up the valley.'

'Well, the new lads'll just have to hold on. Georgie boy was right, wasn't he?'

'Christ, what's that?'

One of the officers pointed down the slope. 'Look, on the track beyond the trees. What are they doing there?'

The officers and now the men in the slit trenches below the ridge stared in disbelief and horror. Along the track from the ruined village a crowd of people were walking. The black skirts and bright kerchiefs of the women, the vivid dresses of little girls, marked them out.

'Civvies. What the hell? They're mad.'

'They're not. Look behind them. The

bastards are driving them on, using them for cover.'

Half crouching, weapons at the ready, troops in brown were moving close behind the villagers.

The battalion commander gave his orders.

'We're going to have to open fire when they get to the trees.'

'But we can't kill women and children! And that's a Republican village.'

'Don't I bloody know it. And so do the fascists. That's why they're using them as cover.'

The troops in the positions overlooking the track through the trees were suddenly motionless with horror and fear, sweaty hands gripping and loosing the hot metal of rifle breeches. Without a word between them, they knew what would be asked of them, in minutes, in seconds.

'Hey. Stop that man. Where's he …' The company commander's voice died away.

'It's Morris.'

From his position in the ridge, throwing his rifle down, and clutching two grenades in his fists, the small figure of Morris appeared on the lip of the trench then launched itself on a wild zig-zag run from rock to rock down towards the lower boulders and the tree line. From behind their human shield the enemy troops opened fire. Spurts of earth and shards of rock sprang from the hillside as George dodged and leapt, now sideways, now downwards but always heading for the treeline.

Then he was through the trees, skirting the group of villagers in a great fifty yard arc, to come looping round in the rear of the Franco troops. Some detached themselves from the group and fanning out ran towards him.

George stopped in his tracks, turned in the dust like a fielder. Thrusting the first grenade to his mouth, he drew out the pin with his teeth and then holding it, holding it seconds more, he threw in a great curve – once, twice, the grenades burst in the air behind the troops. In sudden, mass confusion, they threw themselves down, the women and children scattered blindly for rocks and trees, and from the hillside came the drumroll crash as the Brigaders opened fire.

17 Tod

George opened his eyes. The smell of straw and manure and burning baffled him. Where was he? Beneath his back he felt bare boards. Level with his face was a small, dirt-crusted window in a thick stone wall. Inside his head was the throb and beat of massive pain.

Then he remembered – the charging Franco troops, the hate-filled face, the bayonet point at his throat and finally the reversed rifle butt smashing on to his head.

A face looked down on his – handsome, dark-eyed, moustached. Below it a pair of shoulders in neat uniform, the tassels of an officer, smart belt and pistol holster.

'He is awake. We can begin.' The voice was Spanish, but George knew the meaning. He knew what was to begin. But not yet. The officer had time, it seemed.

'You are a brave man, though stupid.' The officer could speak English.

'They all say that,' George tried to get up,

but from behind him he was seized roughly and slammed down again onto the boards where he lay.

'You will need a sense of humour too.'

The officer moved away and stood by the door.

'We need to know how many men you have on the ridge. We think we know, but we need to be sure. We think one more push will take us over the top.'

George swung his body suddenly to the side, fell from the board ledge on which he lay and landed on the ground. Two men moved towards him, but the officer who was looking through the stable door to the outside, suddenly waved his hand. The two men stopped. George stared at them. Powerfully built, both were stripped to the waist. Their pants were hidden by large aprons.

'Cor, are you going to do the washing up, mate?'

One of the men raised his muscled arm. But the officer now turned round and spoke.

'Very pleasant. But a waste of time, I think. You know why they wear these. It is because they do not want blood and other filth on their uniforms when they get to work. They are good at their job. They like to do it and get to their supper. We have about an hour before supper, I think. Quite enough to find out all that you can tell us. You are a bold man, but not I think a man of importance. Men of importance do not do such things as you did.

'We shall proceed like this. I shall ask you questions and you will answer them. If not, then they will have a few minutes with you. I shall go outside. Then I shall start my questioning again. Each time, unless you tell me what I need to know, the intervals will become longer and longer.'

Without moving his head, George tried through half-closed eyes to size up the situation. So there were three of them. He listened. No one outside. They must be close to the front – in some farmhouse. If he could ...

The officer was amused.

'That is the second stage. At first people are baffled. "Where am I? What is going to happen to me." Then the second stage. "Can I get out of here before they begin to burn my flesh, and break my bones?"'

George looked round again. Now he placed the burning smell. At the farther end of the stable stood a brazier with red hot coals. The thought flashed through his mind – stupid, that, to have a brazier in a stable full of straw, the whole lot might go up. Then he laughed at himself.

'Your name is George Morris. You are with the British Battalion of the International Brigade. You are not a prisoner of war. Mercenaries do not enjoy the protection of the Geneva Convention. We will do with you as we like. If you tell us what we need to know, you may escape being shot. You may live to spend many years in our prisons. But even many years in our prisons will be preferable to an hour in this stable.'

George did not answer.

'I will go outside,' said the officer. The two men moved in closer. George fought them for a while. He could not help himself. But it did not last long. Fifteen minutes later, the officer came back into the stable, and they brought back life into his naked, bruised and burnt flesh, by throwing water in his face.

They stood him on his feet. Something prevented him from fainting again. He wanted to see what was happening. The questions began again, and for the second time the officer went outside and the sickening stench and pain plunged him into darkness once more.

It was at the third time, that the walls of the stables suddenly shook as in an earthquake. The window fell in and a shower of rocks and stones flew across the space. George's two torturers threw themselves to the ground.

Deliriously he mocked them, calling them obscene names. Then suddenly on a mad inspiration he staggered over the straw filled floor, snatched up a wood spar and shoved the brazier over, scattering red coals. As he turned expecting the torturers to grab him again, another massive blast made the stable walls shiver.

He was alone. And he knew why. From his split and blackened mouth came an exultant cry.

'The sods are bombing their own side!'

The sudden crackle of flames as the straw blazed into life around him, quelled his pain-drunk excitement. He snatched up the ragged remnants of his uniform from the ground and staggered blindly out of the burning shed.

18 Fee

Meg came to The Hall as the sun was setting and found Lord Horden and Peverell at supper. The two men did not appear to notice how late she was. Both were in good humour. Both had been drinking.

'What do you say, Meg,' called her father as she entered the room. 'In seven days time, the water will flow the length of the new cut. We shall celebrate that, we shall celebrate your wedding, and ...'

He paused, '... we shall celebrate Mr Peverell's plans for the first drift mine on the lower slopes of Borley ... we'll call it The Lady Margaret.'

She took her seat and smiled at Peverell who had been standing in silence. She knew what he was thinking. He was watching her face to see if she were angry at the use he had made of the rock samples in her collection.

She looked at both men, and raised her glass. 'I too shall celebrate.'

Next morning the portrait painter shook his head. 'The blue dress, Milady, the blue dress. This one is green ...'

'The blue dress is being repaired. Besides, you can make blue green, red yellow, black white if you wish.'

He shrugged. 'Well, we shall do our best. But your face has changed again.'

'How do you mean?' she said quickly, suspiciously.

'You are – in – a calm fever, Milady.'

'Ah, that is the thought of my betrothal.'

He took up his brush.

Late that afternoon, Meg took the blue dress from out of the closet, brushed it down, mended a few tears. She would not let her maid see this. Putting on the dress she stole out so quietly that only the young groom saw her cross the estate wall.

As the sun dipped low behind Borley, she met John Maguire in the hollow. She took off her dress and hung it on the flowering thorn bush and lay down naked with him in the heather. And when they had made love and rested in each other's arms, he told her.

'In four days' time, I'll have all ready. You must leave at dark. Tomorrow I'll bring a boy's jacket and breeches for you. It's twelve miles to the coast. We can make it before dawn. A fisher will take us to Ireland and once in Cork City, I have a friend, an old friend, who'll get us aboard a ship for Australia.'

'And the captain,' added Meg, 'shall marry us.'

'God bless you, Meg.'

Days passed, suns rose and set, the water crept along the deep cut towards the town. Each day Meg stole out to the hollow on the moors, and each evening she supped with her father and Peverell and talked of plans for the future.

And each time she would say, 'I have so many plans for my wedding, but I shall keep them secret.'

And on the fourth day, after sunset, she excused herself from supper, went quietly to her room, wrapped a few belongings together with the blue dress and tied them in a bundle, put on the shirt, breeches and jacket John had given her and stole away to the broken topped wall across the park.

There in the dark she waited, one hour, then two. But Maguire did not come. And when the moon was up she went as quietly back to her room. A cold fear and despair had suddenly taken hold of her. Changing into a dress she sank down on to the bed and tried to think what she must do. Something had gone wrong. Yet she did not know how to find Maguire. She dared not go to the navigators' camp on the edge of the town. That would be folly. All she could do was wait until the next afternoon and hope to meet him in the hills.

A knock came at the door.

'His lordship wishes to speak with you, milady.'

'Tell him I am not well.'

There was a moment's silence.

'He says you must go down.'

Rising quickly she flung open the door. The frightened servant had already run from outside. Striding down the passage she flung open the farther door and hurried down the stairs. Lord Horden sat alone. The supper dishes had been taken away.

'What does this mean, father?' she demanded. 'You have never spoken to me like this before.'

He stood and came around the table to halt a few paces from her. His eyes gleamed.

'No, I have not. And perhaps it had been better if I had done.'

'I do not understand you. Last night, compliments, toasts, plans. Tonight, this.'

'Ah, yes. Last night I did not know what I

know tonight. Last night I did not know my handsome, wilful blue-stocking daughter played the whore ...'

Anger suddenly took the words from her mouth. He went on, 'Played the whore with an Irish ruffian from the navigators' gang.'

She found speech. 'You insult a man you do not know.'

'Ah, but I shall know him better. He did not meet you tonight, because he's in the town jail.'

Lord Horden rapped on the table top. The door behind him opened. Two men entered. First the vicar, then, Meg stared at the second figure, baffled for a moment until she recognised the face of Marker, the man Maguire had rescued her from in the plantation those weeks ago.

'We have a witness to your doings, milady.'

She looked at Marker with contempt. 'I will not speak any more of this while that villain,' and she half turned to the vicar, 'and that spy, are in the room.'

Lord Horden raised his hand. The vicar nodded to Marker and the two left the room again. When the door was closed, Lord Horden took his chair again.

'Maguire was not careful enough with his

plans. We know what you meant to do. But all's not lost. Peverell is – a realistic man. He will not pass up a good business arrangement. He never has.'

'I'll not marry Peverell.'

'Oh, but you will. Because you will not say no to what I will offer you.'

'Offer me?' She was incredulous.

'Yes. You will renounce Maguire. Maguire will be shipped back to Ireland. He'll not be employed over here by any company again. We shall tell those people who suspect that this man Maguire pestered you under pretence of helping you. That he made play with your generous nature. The whole county knows you are a warm-hearted girl.'

'Suppose,' she burst out, 'suppose I have Maguire's child in me. What will you and Peverell do then?'

He did not change his expression, though the light in his eyes was colder and more cruel.

'We shall see. If need be, we can dispose of the child. You're young. There'll be time for more. It'll prove you're not barren at the least.'

'Why you're a fool, Father. One to think that this story can be believed. And a fool to believe I'll lend my name to this mess of lies and treachery.'

He stood up, throwing back his chair with a great crash.

'No, you're the fool, milady,' he shouted. 'If you do not do every thing that I tell you, Maguire will be charged with rape at the next assizes and he'll hang.'

19 Fee

Meg heard her father's words with only part of her mind, as though she had by chance overheard a strange and fateful conversation between two other people. A wave of dizziness swept through her head. She swayed on her feet and caught at the table edge.

Lord Horden took one look at the drained white of her face above the vivid colour of her dress and turning shouted for the servants. But even as the door opened, Meg had forced herself upright, and launched into sudden violent movement.

The maid who had entered was thrust on one side so that she fell as Meg ran out into the passage.

'Stop her,' yelled her father.

Servants appeared in the passage, staring as Meg, dead-pale and wild-eyed rushed past them. Some awkwardly moved forward as they heard their master call, but none stood in her way.

As her father reached the door of the room, the vicar behind him like a dog at heel, she was out of sight. The dull thump of the outer door sent him into a rage.

'Damn you idle, cowardly ...' he ranted. The servants fell back as he stormed forward. 'You, and you, get lights. You, call the groom, get horses ready. She can't go far.'

Outside in the dark, lit fitfully by the moon as the great banks of cloud were parted by night winds, Meg hesitated a moment, then ran, sure-footed across the grass. Behind her lights flashed in The Hall, the noise of shouting grew.

The moonlight suddenly faded, she found herself struggling in bushes at the farther side of the park. She was near the wall, but not on the moorland side. She turned on the run and saw torches flare near the stables. More shouting. Soon they would be mounting and scouring the park. She pressed on through the undergrowth which became thicker as she came to the edge of the estate. Then she was against the rough stone surface of the wall, with a shock that drove the breath from her.

Heart thumping, salt sweat stinging her eyes and running into her open mouth, she scrabbled with feet and hands at the wall. She felt the gown rip as she reached the top, and lay there, gasping hoarsely. The sound of hooves and shouting came closer and riders with torches galloped by on the driveway to the outer gates. Another wave of dizziness turned the light in her mind to darkness for a moment and she rolled and fell from the wall, her body thudding on to the grass slope below.

She dragged herself upright and went forward blindly, now no longer knowing which way she went.

The ground dipped suddenly. She tripped and rolled again, grabbing at bushes, thorns tearing at her hands and arms. Standing again she staggered on, a nightmare blankness in her mind. Now the lights and shouting were to left and right. They were forcing their way towards her from either side. From far, far away she heard her father call her name.

'Meg!'

Clouds rolled away from the moon and its cool white light caught bushes and trees around her. In front, right under her feet, was blackness. She was poised on the edge of the canal cutting. Below the lapping water called her. Footsteps crashed in the brush around her, lights coming nearer as her body rocked to and fro on the crumbling edge of the cut.

She was falling.

20 Roller

Above Kwame's head, the guard's trigger finger tightened, then relaxed. An evil grin came on to his face. Suddenly viciously he stabbed downwards with the musket barrel at Kwame's head.

But in that moment's hesitation, Kwame's arms, linked by the heavy chain, jerked upwards, by reflex. The musket barrel thrust aside, burst into noise and flame. The force of the firing sent the unprepared guard backward. Kwame rose with him and balanced on his toes, clenched hands above his head and brought the chain down on the guard's neck and shoulders. The man collapsed at his feet. Around him was a confusion of yells from the other guards.

'Shoot him!'

'No, hold your fire. Get him.'

Kwame stopped and flung back the guard's jacket. He snatched the man's knife from his belt and then bent again, to tear at the last link of his ankle chain. With all his strength he heaved at it, but the link held. He had no more time. Leaping away, the chain, loose, hanging and jerking at his leg, he ran down the line of crouching, half-awake slaves.

'Where is he? Bring the lamp!'

'He's gone down where the women are.'

'After him.'

Kwame dodged round the bushes and hurled his way into the clearing where the women and children lay.

'Nkansa,' he gasped, breath like fire in his throat.

'Kwame,' she rose up like a shadow just by him. He bent, slashed the rope which linked neck, wrists and ankles, then taking her by the arm, dragged her away into the trees, as the first guards, torches and muskets held up, appeared on the other side of the clearing.

Now she ran alongside him and ran faster too, for all the weight of the child she carried inside her. The loose chain thrashed his legs and ankles like a club, he felt the broken link bite home and draw blood. Bending he tried to gather up the chain, but could not run upright. Crouching, weaving in and out of the bushes, he struggled to keep up with her.

'Uphill,' he called. 'Uphill.'

They struggled up the slope and now they

heard the sounds of their pursuers in the lower bushes. He fell. She took him round the waist and hoisted him to his feet again. She went ahead and took his arm, dragging him upwards while he crouched and stumbled, holding up the imprisoning chain.

They were nearing the top of the first ridge above the forest track and here the trees were thinner. Below they could see the lights advancing.

'Come.' She pulled him forward again. But now the strain of his efforts to free himself and Nkansa, were telling on him. His legs and arms grew wearier.

They stopped again. He made a decision.

'Nkansa. Listen. Go that way, up the hill. Go until you find the Maroons. I will keep them from finding you.'

'No, Kwame. I won't leave you.'

'Yes. You must. Do not let our child be born a slave. Take it. Take it. Go.'

He thrust her with all his might into the bushes up the slope, thrust her so hard that she almost fell.

'Go, Nkansa.'

He listened until he knew he was alone, then turned and began to crash down the slope, shouting as he went, abusing the guards, screaming insults at them. Below the lights swung in his direction. A musket boomed and he heard the shot tear into a tree a few yards away from him.

'We want him alive,' came the shout.

Kwame turned and headed for that voice. He came down off the slope in a great sliding rush, hurling the guard who had shouted off his balance, plunging him down towards the track where the slaves huddled together and, watched by the remaining guards, waited in excited, frightened silence.

'He's heading your way. Let him go, he can't go nowhere that way.'

Kwame stumbled on, working crab-wise across the line of the slope, climbing again. The lights behind and around him formed a half circle. They were pressing in, like a noose draws tight. They were used to hunting runaways. They began to laugh.

'Soon get him now.'

'If he don't go over the cliff.'

'He won't. Don't worry. We'll have him.'

The trees gave out onto a broad grass platform. Kwame stopped and dropped to his knees. Before him a darker darkness showed him that the ground gave way and plunged down. They were close behind him now. He could not get away. He grinned to himself and counted the lights. He had drawn them all away. Nkansa and the child now had their chance.

Now they came on to the platform and stood a few yards from him. Kwame held out both arms, fingers curved upwards, in a challenge as he has seen the sailors on shipboard do when they wrestled.

'Come on,' he called, in English.

'He wants a bout, Jack. Go on, go get him. Don't break him up too much.'

The biggest guard put down his musket and as the others held up their lanterns filling the grass circle with light, he moved forward arms wide. Kwame backed away. The other came on. He backed once more. The guards jeered.

It was too late when they realised what was to happen. A sudden grappling rush joined the two together, then Kwame staggered, holding his enemy in an iron grip. As the two swung and fell into the darkness below the cliff edge, they heard his ferocious shout of triumph.

21 Tod

Towards sunset, the guns fell silent. The bombers headed to the south their work done. They had killed soldiers and farmers, they had smashed trenches and farmhouses, they had wounded many. But the front had held. The raw Brigadiers had had their first taste of war. Some would not live to tell how it felt. But others had survived and knew what it was like to feel fear, to fight it and to hold it at bay, like the enemy. Now all, dead, wounded and the rest lay still in the quiet of the evening, while orderlies brought up stretchers, while food and water was passed down the line. Commanders took stock, counted their men and talked in low voices of the morning to come and whether their thin line could stand another day of shock and strain like this.

Two miles in the rear of the front, beyond the low hills across the valley, two farmers, father and son drove their sheep along a narrow lane in the gathering twilight. They were taking the chance to get their dwindling flock to safety now that the fighting had stopped for the night.

Ahead of them the flock divided on the road. Something lay there and the sheep picked their way neatly round it. It looked like a heap of sacking, a broken bag of corn, or ragged clothing thrown away or…

'Miguel. What's there?'

'It's a man, Father.'

'Let me see. It's a soldier. Look at the belt.'

'See his face, his chest, Father.'

'But how did he come here? The fighting's two miles that way.' The old farmer pointed to the south.

'He must have died running away. I'll roll him in the ditch.'

'Wait, son. He is not one of theirs. He's from the Republican side, that uniform.'

'That can't be. How can he be here?'

'I do not know, but he shall not lie in the road. Son. Run home and get the cart. I'll wait here and keep watch, but hurry.'

The light had almost faded when the mule cart brought the body into the courtyard of the little farm. The women gathered round, clicking their tongues.

'So small. See. He's been burnt. What pigs did that?'

An older woman took charge. 'Carry him inside. We'll wash him clean and put a sheet round him. Think of his mother. How she would feel.'

Miguel and his father had sat down to supper in the light of the lamp for it was now quite dark outside, when his sister Teresa burst into the room.

'That soldier – the soldier ...'

'Yes, the soldier, what of him?'

'He is alive. He opened his eyes and looked at me.'

Next day, long before dawn, Miguel and his father cleared a small space in the loft over the stable. They took fence boards from the orchard and walled in the space, save for a little open part at one end. Then they piled hay and straw against the boards to hide it. After that, slowly and gently, they carried the half-dead soldier and laid him on a matress in the hideout.

And each day after that, morning and evening Teresa took food and water up to the loft and tried to get the man to eat and drink. At first he could not, or would not, but rolled his head and struggled feebly when she tried to hold him up. His body grew so thin and light that she could easily raise him when she needed to wash him. She took away his ragged shirt and trousers and mended them. And often when her work was done before the evening light went she would sit and watch his face.

Sometimes he would dream wildly, mutter and rave. She could not understand what he said, but guessed that he was English, one of the volunteers. No one at the farmhouse spoke to anyone in the village about their guest. Not everyone could be trusted.

Twice soldiers and police came into the village looking for Republican suspects or hidden weapons. Franco's troops were on the offensive now and the front line had moved some thirty miles to the south. Gradually there was quiet and the soldiers went away. But they dared not move the sick man. He was under their protection now and they would not surrender him even to save their own lives.

And if anyone in the family had dreamt of such a thing, Teresa would not have permitted it. Her parents shook their heads as they watched her go each day with mending or embroidery and sit with their uninvited guest in the loft hideout.

He was quieter now. He no longer dreamed crazy dreams and arched his body and tried to crawl out of the tiny space where he lay. He took water and thin soup and when Teresa took his hand and held it, sometimes he would clutch at her fingers in the way a child does. It pulled at her heart. Sometimes he would look at her, but did not seem to see anything.

Her friends in the village became suspicious when she did not join them. She made excuses. The young men became jealous. She laughed at them. But her life was now all within the farm, with her work, and her evening hours with the silent, strange, perhaps mad, young soldier. What had they done to him and why, she wondered, as she bathed the thin body and treated the slowly healing burns and wounds. Who was he? Where had he come from? Would he ever be able to tell his story? What, she thought, what will I do, if his mind has gone and he will not talk like a man, again? She knew the answer. She would nurse him.

'What's your name?'

At the sound of the voice from the thin, cracked lips, at the comic accent of the Spanish words he used, she stared, then started to laugh and cry at the same moment.

He took her fingers in his. 'Don't … don't …' He did not know the word for cry. Teresa leaned down and hugged the bare, bony shoulders. The tears ran down her cheeks.

'I'm Teresa,' she sobbed.

He pushed her shoulders gently, so that he could look into her face. The eyes she saw, were clear. It was as though he saw her for the first time.

'My name's George.'

'George,' she repeated.

'You're Teresa.'

Suddenly, with an enormous effort he struggled up and grasped her arms. 'I know. I've – dreamed it – you're Teresa. Our son ...'

'Our son?' She gazed at him in amazement.

'He'll be called Sebastien ...'

His eyelids drooped. He lay back and fell asleep, leaving Teresa staring into the dusk of the little stable room.

22 Time Annexe

'They have re-entered the Neutral Zone, Medway.'

Jonas, the younger scientist turned from his seat by the control panel as his older colleague entered. The two nodded to each other. They were beginning to work together more easily. But Medway was strangely reserved and would only use surnames. He nodded and sat down silently next to Jonas, while both men watched the screen where the three figures materialised into their silent mist-filled waste-land world.

Abruptly Medway brought the right-hand screen into play. 'Look.'

In the chamber next to the control room, Kera was lying half on, half off the bed and the clothes had been flung to the floor.

'Again we get the same agitation. But there is no sign that Kera is Returning.'

'She must be deeply involved with this other girl.'

'Involved, trapped, impossible to tell.'

'What can we do?' demanded Jonas, as he took in the seriousness of the other's words.

'We can do a number of things, each equally risky.'

'But ...'

'But, my friend, we shall do what the Director decides ... It is his experiment.'

Jonas was suddenly indignant. 'That gives him no right to use her like that.'

'Don't be touchy. Kera is a volunteer, remember. But while she is under experiment, the Department, the Director, must have the final say.'

'I see, the power is his.'

'The power is his, and don't forget it. Unless the Controller overrules him ...'

'In which case?'

'In which case, Jonas, we had better not discuss it. Now be a good chap and call up a helper to settle Kera comfortably again and let us get back to our work.'

As Jonas came back into the room, the screen monitoring the sleeping girl was blank again. Medway, grey-haired head hunched into his narrow shoulders, was watching the centre picture.

As Jonas sat down beside him Medway said without turning. 'See how they greet one another – hugs, kisses, like old friends.' There was a sudden warmth in his voice. 'A shared experience can make a friend for life, you know, if it matters enough.'

'Perhaps,' said Jonas, hesitantly, 'oh, no, it's not ...'

'Go on. You were about to speculate on something. Speculations should always be shared with colleagues. Speak out.'

'They may have become friends in the Neutral Zone. Or they may already know each other.'

'From the past? An impossibility.'

'No, from the future. From our time.' Jonas went on, more hesitantly. 'These two boys have either blundered into Time Track in their own life. Or – ' he lowered his voice, 'suppose they entered the Track from our time. If so, who are they – now?'

Medway smiled.

'If these Intruders have entered the Track from our time, they are either people in this Centre, people from Science City. Or they are Outsiders, from the Old City ...'

'If they are,' said Jonas eagerly. 'Who are they? How did it happen? Why?'

'You may well ask? How do we check? There are no records of birth or death in the

Old City for the past twenty five years.'

'Amazing,' said Jonas. 'Yet our world lives by recording – the unimportant, the trivial.'

'Ah yes,' answered Medway. 'But after the upheaval, after the Civil War, there was an unspoken understanding. Old City people were to be left alone, unrecorded, to live or die, flourish, starve as they wished. A sort of freedom. The kind of freedom our Government believes in. Only one department is interested in Outsiders ...' he paused.

'Reset Security.'

Jonas nodded. 'So, if our Experiment showed there were some kind of contact between our City and the Old City?'

'I don't care to think about that,' said Medway hurriedly. 'Now, be a good chap and call the director. Tell him Kera is back in the Zone. Just that, eh?'

The young man stared a second, then nodded. As he moved to the door, Medway, turned to the panel and began to make audio contact with the Zone.

23 The Neutral Zone

Fee, Tod and Roller sat together, on the rough grass, back to back, their feet stretched out, supporting, warming one another with their bodies, in contact again, in grateful silence. At last Fee spoke, very quietly.

'I've seen so much, I'd like to tell you both, but I can't just yet. It's like a dream, fading away, though I know it'll come back. It's like something I've lived through myself. Not easy to remember. But impossible to forget.'

'Right,' nodded Roller. 'You know, I can't work out how we came here, but it seems right. It's like something I've wanted all my life. Something I've wanted to know, even without knowing.'

Tod was silent. At last Fee turned and looked sideways at him.

'You're not saying anything, Tod.'

Tod lowered his head so as not to meet her eyes, and after a while spoke in a low voice. 'I got here because I ran away from – where I was, you know, present time …'

'Present time, man, you must be joking. This is no time,' said Roller.

'You know what I mean,' answered Tod. 'I mean 1988. That's present time, isn't it? That's us. Even if we swing, back, forwards, that's still us. We've got to be someone.'

'Yeah, Tod, go on.'

'That's the point. I know now what I was so wound-up about. I could have ki…' he stopped as though he remembered something he could not talk about, then went on. 'I was ashamed of who I thought I was. When you're an orphan you're who other people say you are. And I thought I was someone who had to be taken off a drunken, mad, filthy old man and put in care.'

Fee turned again and touched Tod's cheek with her hand. 'Look, Tod, we made a rule, we three. No one has to tell anyone anything they'd rather keep to themselves.'

'No, you've got me wrong. You've got me wrong. I don't mind talking about it now, because I know about him. I know about him. He was for real. He was a man.'

Tod drew up his legs and stood on his feet looking down at the other two who gazed up at him wide-eyed.

'That's why I want to go back – back to our

time, I mean. There's things there I want to sort out. There's things there I thought I couldn't face. But I can now, whatever it costs.'

'You mean, you don't want to make the Time swing again?' Roller had disbelief in his voice.

Tod shook his head. 'No mate. I don't need to. Where I want to go now is going to be great enough for me. How does it go … Know who you were, understand who you are, decide what you're going to be. Well, I've gone through the first part, I'm into the second and I'm ready for the third.'

'Wish I were so sure,' said Roller. 'Tell you what though. I've found out something that's maybe useful.'

'Like what?'

'Like how to be angry. Angry enough to kill someone.'

Tod stared. 'You don't know what you're talking about, mate. That's crazy.'

Roller steadied himself with both hands on the grass and slowly hoisted his body up, to stand hands on hips, above Tod.

'Not so crazy, when you know that being cool, taking it all calmly, letting the world go by, can cost other people their lives.'

Tod looked up at the tall black lad and

nodded slowly. 'That's funny, Roller, mate, because I've been learning the opposite. What's the difference, then? Why?'

'You see, Tod,' Fee was on her feet now, her hand grasping Roller's arm. 'You don't know all there is to know yet.'

'Right,' added Roller. 'Look, I'll tell you. I left people I love, a child not born. I want to know what's happened to them, all that time ago, all those miles away. How did they live, how did they die? I want to go back there. I'm going back there. Just the moment they clear the way.'

'Huh, how d'you know they will?'

'Because I think someone out there,' Roller swept round with his hand, 'someone out there needs to know as much as we need. What do you say, Fee?'

Fee's eyes clouded, a look of pain came to her face.

'I must go back. Yet I don't want to. I came here first because I ran away from a choice I had to make. When I travelled back on the Time Rope, I found there's no escaping from choices, from love, from pain, from people. Husband, father, lover, child ...'

Tears appeared for a second on her cheeks below her eyes. She touched them with her fingers. 'I could not stand the pain, the misery. I escaped. And now I know I must go back. There are things that have to be done. So I shall go.'

Roller rested a hand on both their shoulders. 'Look, I don't really know you two. There's things you've done you don't want to talk about. But we agreed. You don't need to say. Maybe my problem was I'd done nothing that really counted to me or anyone else. But listen. Don't let's split up.'

He drew a breath.

'When you travel time, you travel alone. But this is one place where we have been together. And that counts for me. We've been together. And that's been good. I don't want to lose that. I'm making another journey, but I'm coming back here, hoping you two will be here.'

'I will,' said Fee, warmly, 'whatever happens, I will be back.'

They looked at Tod. He made a face.

'OK, you two do what you feel you have to. I owe you this, because it's happened when I've been with you two. So, I'll make one more trip. I don't know where, and I don't much care – a good, long swinging trip. And then, I'm going home to our time.'

'Whenever that is?'

'Whenever that is!'

'So that's agreed,' grinned Roller. 'We meet here again, we stick together.'

'We do.'

Roller raised his hands skywards.

'So, what are we waiting for, Mister. Open up, Open up, Open up.'

24 Open the Time Track

The Director sat at the control panel, Medway and Jonas stood a little away and waited as he scanned the Neutral Zone, then the side chamber, then the Neutral Zone again. He tapped his fingers restlessly, then said slowly, 'There is a strange bond between them. If this encounter is by chance, by accident, then it is incredible, something more incredible than I have witnessed in my career.

'If, however, it has happened, by design, on purpose ...' Jonas drew in his breath. The Director swung round and smiled grimly at him.

'If it were planned by someone, then you two, and I, this Annexe, this Centre, are in some danger. What the threat is, I do not yet know, but my instincts tell me it will put our existence in the balance.'

'What shall we do, then?' asked Medway. Anwar spoke cautiously, 'I think that it is risky, but we cannot be ruled by fear of risk – not as scientists.'

He stood up, and said firmly, 'Open the Time Track. Let the experiment continue.'

Knockouts Series editor: Jane Joyner
Founder editor: Josie Levine

The Salmon Ewart Alexander
Mia Gunnel Beckman
The Cat People Jan Carew
Dark Night, Deep Water Jan Carew
**Don't go near the water* Jan Carew
The man who came back Jan Carew
Dead man's creek Jan Carew
Save the last dance for me Jan Carew
**Stranger than tomorrow* Jan Carew
Lesley's life Lesley Davies
Twist of the knife Terry Deary
Walking Shadows Terry Deary
I met her on a rainy day Terry Deary
Don't dig up your granny when she's dead Terry Deary
The Treasure of Skull Island Terry Deary
The Ice House of Nightmare Avenue Terry Deary
Love Stories Harry Gilbert
A person of bad character John Griffin
Hooked! Michael Hardcastle
Vet in a spin James Herriot
The Lord God made them all James Herriot
**A Northern Childhood: The Balaclava Story and other stories* George Layton
A Northern Childhood: The Fib and other Stories George Layton
Time Rope *Robert Leeson*
Time Rope: Three against the World Robert Leeson
Time Rope: At war with tomorrow Robert Leeson
Time Rope: The Metro Gangs attack Robert Leeson
A Taste of Freedom Julius Lester
**Long journey home* Julius Lester
Accident Margaret Loxton
At the sign of the Dog and Rocket Jan Mark
The Sheene Machine Andrew Marriott
It's only rock 'n' roll Alan McLean
The Ghost of the Glen Alan McLean
Hostages Kenneth McLeish
**Odysseus Returns* Kenneth McLeesh
Will of Iron Gerard Melia
Silvertown Disaster Gerard Melia
**Journey to Jo'burg* Beverley Naidoo
Fair Fight Barry Pointon
Waves David Rees
Nasty! Michael Rosen
**The Bakerloo Flea* Michael Rosen
Pickled onions Chris Shepherd
**The trouble with Lindy's liftshaft* Andy Smith
The Midwich Cuckoos John Wyndham
Home Truths: Three plays
Picture story book: *Cave Rescue and other stories* Josie Levine

*Cassette available